Wall

Wall

Jen Craig

PUNCHER & WATTMANN

First published in 2023
Published by Puncher and Wattmann
PO Box 279
Waratah NSW 2298

https://www.puncherandwattmann.com
web@puncherandwattmann.com

ISBN   9781922571618

Cover design by Bettina Kaiser
Typesetting by Morgan Arnett
Printed by Lightning Source International

 A catalogue record for this work is available from the National Library of Australia

NATIONAL LIBRARY OF AUSTRALIA

for dad

I

I need to tell you that once I'd given up on the idea of turning the contents of my father's house into a vast and meticulous installation in the style of that famous artist Song Dong, it just took me getting the call from City Hire Skips as I was walking down the hill from the ridge where I was staying – this call that confirmed the bin would be arriving by one pm – to make it seem, suddenly – magically – as if the entire house were already clear of the junk and disintegrating remnants of more than fifty years of abject living, and that now there were no more distractions keeping me from the Wall. Nothing at all between me and this Wall I'd been planning to construct for well over a decade now, as you know – this Wall that, according to all the proposals and applications and descriptions I'd been putting in my CVs and artist's statements since 2002, intends to give "strong and substantial form to a very personal phenomenology of surviving anorexia". And so this Wall that, as you know very well, I have been doing nothing but talking and writing about. Just talking and writing. Because it seemed, then, that by going all out to do the very *opposite* of what my most trusted instincts were urging me to do, the Wall might be possible – this definitive Wall – since now I would be able to jettison everything that needed to be jettisoned, no matter how cruel I would feel as I did it. Hiring a skip only takes a second, I was telling myself over and over in some sort of automatic echo of what *you* had been trying to tell me earlier, Teun. In fact, I was feeling good, so utterly cheered by the knowledge that I had made this radical decision about my work and my life that, as I was walking back down the hill from the shops near the Airbnb with my most recent haul of sponges and liquids (and a brand new bucket and a squeegee mop), I was also noticing how easily the branched reflections of the sky were sliding over the chrome and glass and duco surfaces of the cars that were parked nose to tail along the street. And really, although it still felt dangerous to have done what I did by calling that number and booking a skip – and so setting in motion this decisive undoing of everything that has been blocking me from making this major work, the Wall of "Still Lives" – my ten-metre *surviving anorexia Wall* – for the moment all I had, after the series of confusions that followed that meeting with Eileen in Newtown, was the farce of what you will call, no doubt when you read all this, my *susceptibility* to Eileen and Max and their anorexic daughter – and of course to Sonya and her supposed splattered body intervention at that public lecture by Nathaniel Lord. The farce, and also the *unfortunate news* about Eileen's shattered femur from the accident on the highway that I still need to tell you a bit more about, or at least to contextualise in a sort of a way. In short, everything that I haven't yet had the courage to describe to you properly. Although it still felt dangerous to be doing all this, the whole of the time that I was walking down the hill to the house from where I was staying, I could also hear that high, exhilarating whistle that you often get in those life-enhancing documentaries about falling or jumping from the doorway of a plane.

You've got to imagine it then. I turned the key, the front door pressed inwards, and something of the pasty, enuretic dark of the house was released into the porch. I nearly bailed on what I was going to do, but a renewed determination made me grab at the edge of the door with the heel of my hand and push it forwards and forwards until I heard something crack. I knew that now I was being uncaring, pragmatic, brutal even – an *unfeeling* daughter, an *unfeeling* sister. Really, I was thinking as I kept shoving at the door, if I hadn't been stumped from the very beginning of this – stumped by how difficult it was to touch anything of what needed to be moved in here – stumped in the way that I have been stumped for most of my life – that if none of this house and what it meant for me had been such a problem or a barrier – and of course a temptation – a very real temptation to the fakest part of me, the one who loves to please – I could *so easily* have made the call to the skip hiring place much sooner than I did. I could have made the call when I sat in the train on the T2 line after I'd booted up the phone with the Aussie SIM card in it. I could have made the call from the underground railway platform in those first few minutes out of the airport, when instead I had succumbed to wave after wave of what I had assumed at the time to be just the first very deep and painful stirrings of excitement about this new kind of work I was about to make – this supposedly all-encompassing major work that would not so much supplement what I have been doing with my piecemeal "Still Lives" project, this tentative Wall, but set it off in the way that it needed to be, by giving it *a greater and more generous cultural context*. So eager was I to be starting on what was promising to be a considerable work after everything I'd been planning on the phone, in emails and in person about the *Chatswood Song Dong project* with Nathaniel Lord.

And so, yes, I concede now, and as I was imagining saying to you while I was shoving at the door – imagining putting to you *somehow* – explaining to you *somehow* – if I had known first up that this idea that had seemed such a perfect idea was *yet another distraction* from what I needed to face in myself, I could have asked some practical questions at the Vodafone desk in the Arrivals hall. I could have asked when they sold me the SIM card, which meant getting one of those rabbit-faced boys to say what *he* would have done here in this city if *he'd* had to clear out a house like this. I could – I knew – have even googled the predicament on the spot when I'd fixed up my phone and then called one of the skip hiring companies while I was still standing there in Arrivals. And so it was with a lift of reckless joy that I pulled the front door to again, so that I might squeeze in behind it and then push myself into the dust and stink of the hallway beyond. So that I might make contact at last with what, after all, had to be nothing more than *random useless shit* – yes, loving these Oz expressions, as you can see – nothing more than a few too many boxes and bags and wires. Nothing but *objects*, as Nathaniel Lord would have called them. To make contact with the rotting, dryish-damp and flaking substances of what I had to keep thinking of as the utterly ordinary leavings of disintegrating cardboard boxes and papers and cords and rusting lengths of fence stakes, which I knew dad would have salvaged from somewhere – so much of it useful still – or at least potentially useful, as dad would have seen it. These only very *sort-of* objects that I had glimpsed when I'd used the torch app on my phone to look through the house after I had pushed my way in from the back not long after I'd arrived in the country, before I'd got around to getting the power connected again. The stark view I'd had of it then – of everything that I feared and that demanded to be taken in, whole, into myself. The whole of its substance. The whole of its abject state. And all of it entirely, without the smallest modification or change. This way I'd thought I was obliged to be filled to the top of myself with the complete material account of what was left of our lives in this house in Chatswood – every last bit of its myriad details and connections, and on a scale unimaginable. The leavings of dad but also of mum, and the rest of us too – the entirety of our lives in this house, as well as those of all of the earlier households and people whose collections we'd made ours from the generations earlier, and so the full textured spread of what I had once got away from as quickly as I could when my anorexia failed. This fearful feeling I have always had that it is either all or nothing with me. All or nothing.

It was in this moment, then, that was still only a few hours before the first of the bins was due to arrive that I stretched out my hands to touch what I could of the stuff in the hall. It was better to do this – to touch it – I was thinking. Touching it first so I could feel and so know that the things I was touching were simply *things* – this stuff that was only inert. Surely. A collection of substances. Nothing more than atoms that had clumped and died, and hence material that could have no inner liveliness. No inner stirrings of its own. Which meant that, although it continued to feel as if I were being faced with the removal of the skin from my body, I pulled what I could of something towards me – some kind of papery substance – a soft, folded remnant of a sheet of newspaper, probably. Something that seemed to have been coated with something else. Something that immediately – even before I could get hold of it properly – left on my hands some thickish residue. Dust, very likely, I was thinking as I felt how it lodged into the whorls of my fingertips, blunting them. Dust, of course, being largely skin.

And so it was with this first definite and intrusive contact that the house was, finally, to disgorge what had long been concealed within: the dry and the dead, the stuck and the foul. The horrendously formless, desiccated bog of disintegrating matter that it still felt too frighteningly wrong to be touching at all. As if, through the decision I had made to get hold of what I could of it, to grab and to shift it, I were already condemning everything in the house – or rather, as if simply through the decision to move it in *any* direction that wasn't into the careful relation of one thing to another – one bit or *object* to another (in the manner of the pre-eminent artist of the resonance of objects: the Chinese genius-artist Song Dong) – or indeed even *into* such a relationship – even *into* the Song Dong sort of vision if it came to me first and easily, which I knew it wouldn't – as if by doing this, I were already destroying everything of value in my life, and in the lives of all of us. Since, as it has always felt to me – and for the whole of my existence – any attempt to change *just how things were* in the precise arrangement of the stuff I'd inherited would be to raze and obliterate it. Raze and obliterate. In fact, it felt as if just by opening the door like this, and with such intentions, I were *already disturbing the evidence* – as if, when I had gone and let loose with that call to City Hire Skips, I had released into the world a menacing presence with a menacing process, and with every move that I made further against the substance in the house, I was breaking, in an ever more serious way – an ever more *unforgiveable way* – an understanding that I had inherited along with my hair, my bones, my teeth. A sacred understanding that, for most of my life, I had only managed to hold on to through the persistence of a pained avoidance and, of course, neglect. This sense that, with the call I had made to the skip hiring place, the testimony of everything here in the house was going to be altered forever – that soon nobody else in the world would have the chance to learn what needed to be learned from this material, which, up to this moment, I had managed to preserve in a sort of a way – and for which I'd *almost* had a plan. *Almost* had a vision for how it might have been kept, preserved and thoroughly understood. *Something will be furious*, I was thinking, then, in the doorway – incoherently thinking. Because what *was* this something? And so my awareness that there might really have been a supra-normal being that was watching me at the doorway – a supra-normal being that was contorted, even, with shock and rage. And yet I knew that it made no sense at all to be trying to imagine this something as a being because it couldn't be a being, surely, I was thinking – not dad's older sister, Beryl, who was beyond such thinking. Beyond such feeling, even, as I'd realised the last time I saw her, when she was pasting those hearts and stars and coloured-in Easter egg shapes onto a green painted box. And not Angus either, since I knew he would have been glad that there was something I was planning to do with the stuff in the house – even glad that what I was going to do with it would *not* involve him. And not any of the "surviving relations", as the lawyer had called them. That is, not Beryl's children or children's children, who preferred to keep an acceptable distance – a coolish, if always very friendly, distance – from any of the troubled muck and disorder of the house (the most I had seen of them being the red tail-lights of a coffee-coloured Land Rover passing by that time when I was sitting out the front on the low brick fence early on, not long after I arrived in Sydney – a Land Rover packed with yellowish dogs – a sense of my *once removed cousin* mouthing something at me as she was passing – perhaps about the dogs she was having to deliver somewhere or other, unless it was some other person I was recognising – some other person from school or art school). Yes, whatever Angus would do, I was thinking as I began to wonder about it a bit more – trying to imagine what he would do or say if he knew what I was planning to do with the contents of the house that I was finding in the doorway here (pulling at these strings or fibres, these flaccid loops of plastic that kept breaking off) – whatever he would do or say, I was having to realise – even if it were a strong reaction – he would rather it were *me* making the decisions. Every one of the decisions. That he would, in fact, do anything at all to avoid having to make a single decision for himself. So often the reactions I have got from Angus about the house or dad have been extreme: a shouting chaos or nothing at all. These two sorts of reactions. And not so very different from the extremes of my own reactions, I was having to realise as well. This Angus who was still only answering my calls and my emails with a flooding of theories about what was happening (which is to say, *failing* to happen) with a woman in Perth – or what rather had failed to happen fifteen years earlier when he had trialled for a time living in the centre of that city on the edge of the Indian Ocean – when he had very nearly got married to *that woman*, as I still think of her. A flooding of theories from Angus – those attempts to join one non-occurrence onto another non-occurrence that made no sense even when I read and re-read his emails or thought over his calls for hours and days. Angus never answering a single one of my questions about dad or the house after dad had died, or indeed anything about the circumstances that had clearly prompted this brother of mine to send that text where he wrote that he needed *to have a break you realise I haven't had a break I can't stand this place and dad and the godawfulsmell any longer.*

Okay, I admit, I was not so much thinking of Angus as the individual that he is, who might still want to be consulted "properly", as you've kept on saying, but Angus, rather, as part of the problem of the house – Angus as just another manifestation of the *overwhelming mountain of things to deal with here*, as I know I've been describing both the house and my absconded brother to you, Teun. Angus and the house, which is to say the frustrating mystery of its vast accretions, which, as I was starting to see in the dark of the doorway, were nonetheless my own accretions as well – my own "problem" with space and clutter, as I know you like to think of the way I'm unable to stop myself filling the rooms where we live in Bethnal Green above that shop you bought in the nineties on Roman Road – my inability to sort, to cull, to "prioritise", as you call it, even with important things. The things that matter. Even with those pieces that I have been making in my supposed preparations for the Wall – my panels of "Still Lives" – those pieces I have been making "obsessively", as you put it – those tiny figures that I "keep placing" in over-wide and cluttered spatial environments – the pressing in of actual substances, too – those figures that I "seem to have such difficulty" placing in and between the layers of perspex and found materials so that they can be seen but also not seen at all. Those projections and holograms. Those palimpsests of media images that I've been texturing into the treatments. Those concentrations of (in)edible substances. Those distortions of figures (and distortions of matter) that I've been driven to put together these last several years for the purpose of "understanding the figure as a material collision of differing perspectives", as I've put it, because *also* as a "substance among other substances", as I have tended to put it as well. And of course, working hard to flog the "crass aspects" of my name, as Sonya has been saying all over Facebook. *Doing nothing but cynically working with what my name suggests. My diet company name.* The name that I prefer to "push", as she sees it, because I don't have a single idea in the world to offer other than this name and all it suggests that we – the always potentially anorexic *we* – are being faced with in an increasingly crass and commercialised world. And yet, even so – and despite everything that I have been resisting in what she has been saying about my supposedly exploitative treatment of the anorexic experience in my work – despite how I've been laughing at it too – so often laughing at it – I have also, as you see, been starting to see that there might *actually* be a connection between what I have been doing all along – or at least failing to do – with my individual "Still Lives" pieces, and my problems with myself, and my problems with this house. My "dithering around" with those pieces, as you like to call what I've been doing, despite the success I have had. *The surprising success* (your words). Never committing myself to what I need to commit to, as you continue to say, because even the abundance of figures a problem – far too many figures. And far too mechanistic a relationship between them and the symbols of culture around us that I have "overly relied on", as you said to me that time I pressed you into saying it. And yet also this way that I've "persisted" in turning down those "generous offers", as you call them, to mount the Wall of "Still Lives" that my proposals have continued to put forwards. Or rather, never being up to making this necessary and definitive version of the smaller pieces that my website keeps pointing to as well. Yes, even with Nathaniel Lord, in Hackney, who tried to get me to talk about it as soon as I spilled that the idea existed. So keen to weasel it out of me, as it seemed – at least until he was lured in, instead, by what we've all come to call the *Chatswood Song Dong project* – that sure-fire, celebrity diversion of a project that I offered very quickly in its place.

And so it was in this moment, then, in this willed entry into the house – in this determined effort to breach the effect of the house without looking too hard at what I was doing – that I started to be aware that I was nonetheless violating something, hewing at something that shrank as I advanced. As if, while I was reaching out and then pulling towards me what I could of it – of these partial handfuls of formless, chafing, and only apparently lifeless, matter – yes, the entirety of what had to have been the strange, clogged world of our lives in this house that had driven my mother, daily, to a taut and frizzed despair. As if, in the very act of reaching and grabbing, I was being forced to see that this same material was not so much furious – furious and monstrous – but actually vulnerable. Infinitely vulnerable. That it was something that needed to be protected and so *always* protected – from *her*, for instance, as I used to see it, which is to say protected from what I would describe as *her inborn tendency to be irritated with everything*, as I think I have said to you on many occasions. Protected from what I have actually described to you as intrusions too – her *many uncalled for and unwanted intrusions* on me, on my world, and – even – and especially – on my *anorexic self*. Yes, I could see that in doing what I was trying to do to the material in the hallway, to this kindly and sensitive world of clutter, of *stuff* – of never dealing with anything that could be left where it was. *Decided on later.* This stuff that I actually remembered defending from what I still thought of as those *needlessly spiteful incursions from my mother* (how I would work to keep her from my own congested space then). I could see that in doing what I was doing in the front doorway of the house, it was as if the whole of this oh so very precious matter was now being pulled limb from limb and hence was – obviously – stirring darkly. So very hurt. Soon outraged. Becoming incensed, of course, that *I* was the one that was doing this violence to it. *I* of all people. Doing this violence to what I should, rather, have been doing my all to soothe and protect. Doing violence to something over which I have tended to shower my most responsive feelings – my most *empathetic* feelings. And so this stuff, which is to say this "rubbish" (*your word*) – yes, the mass of this rubbish that has always had for me such a definite, prior, and intrinsic value – a most astonishingly gentle benevolence and value – protecting this stuff that had once, in fact, been active and helpful in sheltering me from what I had then considered to be the harsh and pitting grey sands of the wastes that were continually being threatened by *her*. The abraded world that *she* would have rolled over everything if she had managed to *have her own way* with our rooms and the rooms of the house that had been "taken over by your father and his crack-headed schemes" – which is to say, rolled over by the pointed serrations of conifers and *edgings* and limitless lawns and the grim sort of concreted mansion she had once hinted that she would have preferred to be living in instead, whether or not we shared it with her. And so the necessity to ensure the survival of this press of warmth against such a soulless expanse. These soft interleavings of the stuff that was yet to be sorted. The whole of it: dust, hairs, feathers, books, papers, candles, pins, badges, sticks, leaves, and so all of the bits – all of the usually annoying bits of nothing in particular that had always scuffed around on the floor in my bedroom – wrappings from lollies, as we call them here, and pen lids. Parts of things that could yet be repaired, at least in theory. Always on the point of being sorted, of course. *I'm just about to sort through that stuff, mum, just leave it, will you.* Never forgetting the tiniest fragment of any of the matter. This confusion of one thing and another, and their intermediary substances. Not one thing only and not yet another, but all of it leaning, and pushing – even being *allowed* to push against me. Yes, the way I must have encouraged it. The huge sloughed wadding of its vital and delicate disorder having become so familiar, so very comforting, because also as alive and as promising as the pressing of green and woody weeds that could never be cleared from the garden. And thus it must have been in this way that the house had grown into its vast amassings, to the despair of my mother, of course, as I could only now get a sense of properly here in the doorway, where I was groping as methodically as I could along the wall for a light switch. Here passing over something smoothish, cold – that had been jammed against the wall. Then something that was shuddering. And then a substance that tore with a slip and a break, like the skin of an animal that has died and then dried and, for a long time now, even ceased to rot. Yes, all of it growing, to my mother's never-to-be-ended despair – never-to-be-ended, since the stroke that had made her die at the centre of its flowering confusion, shoved up hard against what I still see as that place under the kitchen table where there were always those brown-waxed boxes of blackish bananas that my father would have collected from somewhere and then forgotten. Those damp-seeming boxes as well as the fungused insoles of his numerous shoes – all of them flipping like drying slugs as she'd writhed on the floor. My mother unable to do anything but flail all the harder around where dad had always been leaving his things that she "hated seeing everywhere in the place". This way she'd been lying as if she'd just been down there on her knees looking for something among "the incredible state of their kitchen", or so a neighbour had told me at the funeral – my mother's fingers stretching out in the darkness and quivering, he'd said – "still alive" – as if she were trying to grasp, or at least to remember, the thing that continued to elude her (my dad having fetched this neighbour because mum had been "looking a bit strange", as he apparently said). Yes, my mother who, in that moment, was still attempting either to reach the object of her desire or despair, or to have one last and definitive say about the excrescence that could no longer be contained at "his end" of the house. Dying in this house, then, which – after all those years – must have seemed to the neighbours to be as expected and natural as the antics of the possums that dad never caught and which, despite the elaborate convolutions of electric wiring he'd rigged in the garden, still managed to get to each of the supposedly edible peaches – to not leave a single, eventually shrunken, yellow fruit whole. As expected and natural, too, as the pale-stalked bluebells that pushed up through the mountainous piles of fallen leaves from the liquidambars and the matting of that pappy wandering "dew", as I used to think it was called, which clogged, particularly, the far incinerator corner of the yard with its brown bogged hollows of stagnant water and funnel-web spider lairs. This red brick house and its seeming *over*-accumulation of contents, whose warren of secrets I had always known I would need to understand and so take into myself, in some intimate manner. This world of the house and its claims on me that I was going to dismantle and send into the void in a series of skips.

And so I could see that no matter that I had *consciously* rejected the Song Dong approach. No matter that I had made myself face the fact that the Song Dong approach in his much praised *Waste Not* installation was utterly wrong for me and this house – that the house as well as my existence in relation to it was somehow in excess of Song Dong's achievement, and indeed of everything that he might have done had *he*, the master, been here in my place. No matter that I had pushed the Song Dong approach to one side and so deliberately moved on to a "much more sensible viewpoint" – moving on, therefore, to the *serious practicalities* that you, Teun, have been trying to get me to face the whole way along – this stern confrontation with the definite and ordinary thingness of it all. No matter that I had been decisive with the call to the skip hiring place, I could also see that I would have to *force* myself to touch and then grab and shift any more than a tiny fragment of the stuff at any one time. And so it was with a yank of rippling, ripping, rent disgust that I pulled a snarl of what turned out to be several shadings of dust-furred electrical cords from the pile beside the door – a snarl that weighed low. That dragged its monstrous, slippery mass over the rucklings of plastic bags, the lip of the porch, and so down onto the grass where it lay like a kill of cold, skinned snakes on the path. Helpless, wobbling, bitter. I shook with the fright of it. The horror of what I had done. Because I could see that even though I had slipped so easily into this mood of *at last doing something about the house* when I'd made that call to the company with the bins – so glad I had done it, so happy that I had pushed the whole of myself into making that call – everything loosening a little (*and so the Wall imaginable for the very first time*). Even though I'd felt all this promise welling up in me – this sense of at last getting to know what it was, really, to be *post*-anorexic – *a surviving anorectic* – I also had the sense that the freedom I thought I was grasping for myself was not free at all but, instead, precarious. That by pushing – like this – past my "irrational feelings", as you have always called them, I had pushed very definitely in the *wrong* direction. The very *worst* direction. That rather than going in a direction that was far more solid and sure and harmonious and even *normal* – where I thought I was heading – *like everybody else* – where I thought I'd be getting a definite and *normal* overview of everything important that I needed to know in order to understand myself and so make the Wall – that rather than doing any of this, I had only gone and stepped a lot further *away* from the focus of what I needed to do, and to a place that was tenuous, hollow, about to give. Which is to say that even as I was remembering what I hoped to have been my normal-sounding response to the people in the skip hiring company when they had asked me whether I would be "taking delivery of the bin" on the driveway or in the street, I was also remembering that the ground in that moment had seemed to shift – that it had dipped and dimpled under the soles of my shoes, and that there was a hissing sound as if the many small stones that were everywhere on the lawn were now draining slowly in a long quiet line into a hole beneath.

Okay, at this moment, I could see that if, instead, I had come back to Nathaniel Lord that time at the Tate Modern Café with a much more appropriately cautious evaluation of the "Antipodean Song Dong approach to the leavings of post-war suburban anxiety in Australia", as he, the founding owner and curator of Thinkspate Galleries – and my one-time mentor at art school – had described what I had supposedly offered very "definitely" the previous evening in Hackney when he was trying to get me to commit to the Wall. That is, if I had responded with a far more sober and cautious handling of this particularly "inspired and daring" solution, which had obviously impressed him, as I think I had hoped to impress him (this Song Dong solution that was to serve, at least, as an interim for the Wall). Yes, if I had *slowed right down* and admitted that I hadn't yet thought through any of the logistics – any of the details – of this supposedly "amazing" project idea. If I had actually admitted to him what I would have known all along – that is, that I really didn't think I could get it together quite so quickly nor so simply in this single trip as I might have led him to believe. If I hadn't been so *carried away* with what he had relayed back to me in glowing terms – so carried away by what, it seems, I had done in convincing him of the astonishingly well-thought-out brilliance of what hadn't even occurred to me a minute beforehand. If I hadn't been so completely and ridiculously carried off and so "out of myself", as my mother used to call what happens when something like this forms in me through the presence of another – an alien something – the way that I can appear, to people like her at least, to be "so quickly taken over" – so quickly overrun (this whole problem of "the other person" in the mess of it all, as I think I might have tried to explain to you once, or at least after that time in Chester when I stayed up late with your cousin, watching Korean wrestling videos until five o'clock – sprawled on a sofa where the sticky brown foam was pushing through the plastic skin like foul soaked toast – even the beer that I never drank, all drunk – bottles of it – the sugary pickles that I normally abhorred – so "susceptible", as you put it, to the peculiar interests of someone as dominating as your Chester-living layabout Rotterdam cousin – the influence of your cousin who will latch onto anyone who will hear him through). If I hadn't been so taken aback by doing what I had done in convincing Nathaniel Lord. If I hadn't been so thrilled by the effect of this parrying of one overly ambitious project with another. If I'd come right back, instead, to this one-time art school mentor of mine with a much straighter, more direct, more *realistic assessment* of what I'd unthinkingly described when he'd asked me in Hackney *whether I had any other projects on the horizon*, I might not have brought this sheer atavistic terror on me, let alone on Nathaniel Lord himself, who has evidently been crushed by all that has happened since he put out what he did about this planned "suburban vision" for 2020 on social media and his newsletter – crushed, that is, after Sonya had *had her say*, as she still likes to put it in those Facebook posts that Eileen *shares* – so entirely crushed. Because he is not answering any of my messages at the moment. Not even a tweet. Gone quiet.

Weeks of being buoyed along by this Song Dong solution. Then, now – infatuated – obsessed – with the Song Dong solution that had promptly overtaken everything else I had been planning to do – whether about dad and the house or even and especially about the Wall of "Still Lives" that I hadn't, until these last several days, felt ready to face in a serious way. Dad could be like this too, I was thinking as I remembered how *he* had always "carried on", as mum used to call it, with his sudden "brilliant" ideas that would overtake him in a second – the latest of which he would regale – indeed batter, hound – anyone who would listen. Never realising of course in his passion, in his utter conviction, that he was always exaggerating even the more credible of the details – always making outlandish claims. So intent on "getting through to" the listener that the feasibility of what he was saying to them would never get to be tested, and the one important message he was hoping to deliver would get sidelined and laughed at and hence ignored. And so my dad making massive and thus immediately (and clearly) unrealistic claims for what had just taken over his mind for that moment. A situation, which would then press him into drawing all sorts of preposterous connections between one thing and another, and in such a way that it could be foisted on the listener as an all-encompassing solution to everything that needed "fixing" in the world. Stretching and then tightening what he said so that it would do this job of solving every single problem that the listener might possibly ever think of – anything that would help my dad in his mission of trying to get through to the listener with this brilliant and final solution. *And so much like me*, I then caught myself saying out loud in this house as the situation of Max and Lulu came to mind once more. How the scene of my flustering in their kitchen and then in their garden pushed into my thoughts uninvited at the very same time I was trying to feel around on the wall behind and past the piles of stuff where the cords had come from – so that I might feel for that plastic protuberance along the wall – that old-style electrical light switch – which I knew I would recognise and seize the instant I found it. The pain of remembering that kitchen and garden moment. Hating to remember it. Yes, this was where dad and I joined up, I was thinking as I pushed my dead dad forwards again, so that I might see him all the clearer (all this pushing, too, of my fingers over the wall in sort of peppery circles – passing, unsurprisingly, over crusted, crumbling matter). Thinking about the way that dad would persist with what he was driven to say about cancer and comets and aliens and the Rife machine therapy and the usual assortment of medical conspiracies that he would always go on about whenever he set upon telling anybody about them. When just the slightest of cues from a person near him – say, the mildest of questions – a mere politeness – would invariably launch him into any one theory he was itching to describe. Dad and I, I was thinking – appalled as I was thinking it: the two of us always and completely insensible to the discomfort of our listeners. Yes, appalled to be remembering the way I had gone on and on at Max in the mountains after I had seen his daughter in the state she was in. The cue of the daughter. The problem of the daughter (*the anorexic daughter*). Dad and I never taking a hint, no matter how strongly our listeners were signalling, probably, that we were being *way out of line* with what we were saying to them, and so often unfeeling too. Insensitive about the situation of our listeners. Determined to ignore any cue from our listeners – our supposed listeners – our *forced-to-be* listeners. Ignoring what they were probably trying to say or hint – the way they would always, no doubt, be desperate to say or do something *else* the whole time we were immersed in trying to get through to them with the one fascinating piece of information that, as it always seemed, *they needed to hear*. This way, too, we would talk in a continuous and insistent manner that would either break the will of the listener – destroy their composure with the aptness of our message, or try their patience until it slowly wore through. Or – fantastically – always the hoped-for illusion – the possibility that we might succeed in shattering, in an instant, what we had always imagined to be the crusted shell of their hopeless ignorance, and so capturing their hearts and *changing their lives*. Of course, this wasn't such a great thing to be thinking about right now, while I was trying to deal with the leavings of the house – with this foul sort of muck on the wall in the hallway as well. The whole of the immense and undeniable problem of the stuff and its continuing effect on my state of being. And yet it was fascinating too. The way that the house and this mode of talking – dad's, mine – this insistent carrying on – how all of it was fusing into a sort of texture: the thickening texture of our contingent lives. And I knew you would be glad to know that I was doing this, too. Thinking this, even. Thrilled, as I expected you to be, that at last, after all you have said over the years, I was starting to see that I did this – that I *actually* did this. Always battering people but never noticing that I am battering them. Never taking the hint. This "cavalier" way, I might have said (following you), that I have with people, with things, and so with my supposed ideas as well. But wait. I can do more. You have to think of it (here, addressing you in my head): dad and me. How the two of us seemed to have been born to do this – expressly to do this. How *normal* it had always been for us. How we would duck and nod our heads as we talked – talking on and on in this automatic mode that the whole of our beings longed to get into, as if it were only once we got into this mode of talking and being and living that the world could change into a more perfect state. And how in this mode – in this dominating, monomaniacal mode of talking and being – we would thus avoid ever having to deal with even the most recent remnants of ideas we'd left behind us – all of them old, useless and superseded, clearly. These past ideas (or things) that we ourselves had put in their apparently "temporary" places around us for a reason we never got round to discovering, since we were always so busy being "onto" something else. As if each of these remnant pieces of thought – these remnant moments (become remnant things) – were only ever waiting where they were, suspended in the air where we had last divulged them, because they were also "about to be" slotted into a system that we were still developing. Slipped so easily and logically into the one relevant, if soon-to-be-forgotten, single spot in our hoped-to-be compelling explanation that would "solve", as dad always put it, the myriad of serious problems "on our planet" that nobody else in the world had managed to solve. And hence all of this refuse, everything soon to be gathered – always about to be gathered – into the single brilliant system that we were always on the verge of explaining in full. *A Wall*, if you like.

It was while I was still thinking all this about dad and me that I found the switch and pulled it down. This old-style switch. And so now, with the suddenness of a word interrupted – like an impression that slips to one side and is lost – the sick yellow light of the fantastically bulbous incandescent globe that dad had always insisted on using (his "stand" against the dangers of mercury, apparently, as Angus once told me – this "conspiracy of poisoning" unleashed on us by the "climate change fanatics") – yes, with the light from this over-sized globe oozing over the upper skins of everything in the hallway, shrinking them down, and making what I faced in the house so much more rigid and ordinary, I laughed that I had been having such thoughts about dad and me. Becoming shocked, in fact, that it was so easy to do. Since I could see that this type of thinking about the two of us – this generalising, teleological way of thinking about how we were so similar in these few key ways – was, in fact, only one more example, ironically, of his (and my) too readily obscuring ways of thinking, as I thought you would like to know as well. Our ways of joining everything up – *always overlooking the details* – in our hurry to rush a thought through to the one seemingly inevitable action or assertion that its logic would always call forth in us. Because, yes, even this, I was thinking. Even this way I had started so easily to assume that dad and I were essentially the same – that our minds were the same. The same way of thinking. The same way of speaking and not listening to others. Our skins the same. Our fate the same. This dad who had died most improbably from an "upper respiratory infection", as I'd learned from his death certificate when I arrived here in Sydney, and whose features were likely to be still discernible, if I was able to see him lying in his box above mum in the newly turned ground. This dad who was always going on and on about nothing at all very obvious or well accepted, but only the most obscure and controversial of theories – who had never even been "active", as they say, in a community of people who were thinking the same kinds of thoughts, because always on the outer. Banned from meetings (as I heard from mum, from Angus as well) – and of course, never working with people in any way at all. For years and years,

26

working in his solitary office, not trying to *connect*, as I do (I was thinking) with disabled teenagers – "making such a difference", as I am told I
do on so many occasions, no matter that it is hard to see it could possibly be true since I so rarely think of the teenagers when I'm not actually
with them and helping them with their pieces. And so dad working long
and hard, but never with people. Never with those who were nothing but
holes for him to pour his theories into – holes just waiting to be filled – or
else complications to be avoided, or tested, or flattered when he could. His
frequent little jokes about how "wonderful" their houses, the "best" he had
ever seen. And also those who "ridiculed" him, as he so often called it – the
ones he longed to press against a wall "so they could finally see". In fact,
for the most part working *against* people. Always "against the competitors",
he would say, who were trying to "steal his ideas". Working on alone with
the most obscure sorts of computer solutions for his particular line of work
in combustion technology – even in the seventies, the eighties. In other
words, even in an era when no one I knew had ever *heard* of computers, or
only thought of them as chunky adding-up machines. And all those stacks
of slotted, cream-coloured rectangular cards that would be lying around in
the house when I was growing up – those collections from the university
where he'd gone to "pursue" his research. His supposed *solutions*. Those
esoteric and apparently highly successful combustion formulations that he
had coded into a computer system that I never bothered to see for myself
or ask about. Probably ingenious solutions to his workplace problems, then.
Certainly, solutions that had been *lured* out of him, as I later heard. The
whole package stolen by a colleague in the weeks, if not days, before he was
sacked by his boss's wife, who, even though she knew nothing at all about
the business – nothing about combustion engineering or computer technology – had taken over the company when her husband died. "Dumped
by the company", as my mother used to say. Used, abused, and dumped by
the company he had worked for his entire working life. Yes, this is why I
was going to have to do this, I told myself as I looked over the junk in the
hallway – over everything that either dad had left there, or Angus and dad

together. The pathos of these leavings. These appalling leavings that asked me to remember them. Demanded I value them. Asserted their claims.

And so it was that I was able to spot and then pull, from under a scabrous tower of half-empty cardboard boxes, a black plastic garbage bag of what, as it struck me, had to be definite, useless rubbish – *a real bag of rubbish*. After all, it was knotted at the top. Tied off, as I could see, by someone at some time. A bag of rubbish that this same someone – perhaps Angus – had once intended to get out of the house and into a bin. A bag (very light) of bulbous objects that might have been sucked-dry tennis shoes or clumps of knotted rags – if only I could imagine Angus thinking such objects were rubbish – which I knew he wouldn't and couldn't (just as dad wouldn't have either). And so it took my *all* to restrain myself from looking inside the bag, just to check that it was okay to chuck the thing – my all to keep on this mission to do what I was intending to do by clearing stuff like this right out of the house. But then, as I sent the bag sliding down the stairs from the porch and onto the path (where it split as something inside it sliced through the skin), I was struck by the absurd-seeming notion that it would have been *so* much easier *to get past all this* – this painful problem with dad and his leavings – the pathos of his leavings – if only I had been able to see what I was doing in some more sequenced, mechanical way. Like this. The actions of it only. This picking up and twisting and turning and flinging and releasing. And so as a series of ordinary muscular contractions – one after another – not thinking too much but allowing each singular contraction to prompt another. A chain of contractions. Which is to say a kind of way of living or at least *moving* "in the moment", as I have heard it described before. And hence, even, into a series of *mindful contractions*. I then laughed, of course, "mindful contractions" being so much and entirely the kind of thing that Arijit would say, as I am sure you would know – this word "mindful" that he likes using and so trying to get us to catch on to as well. His mindful eating, his mindful working, his mindful listening, his mindful sex – all of it definitely and usefully (apparently) "mindful". That mindful cleaning of his teeth, that mindful walking so that he can mindfully buy the coffee that he will attempt to drink mindfully on his way to work on a day that disperses in "the usual bits and bobs" but nonetheless comes to a head in that moment when, after pressing himself into the crowds on the platform at Bank, he watches a couple mindfully rowing in a New Zealand fjord in a video ad on the wall, and it "brings him back at last", as he says, "to understanding what *really matters*" – where he can finally "centre" himself, since only then does he realise that he is – in that moment – standing on a platform in Bank. And so: *mindful.* Such a term as my auntie Beryl would have used against me if she had known about it before she went gaga and gluey. Always using notions like these against me. If you were doing it *mindfully,* she might have said about one thing or another, it would have been "far more successful". This way she would always be discovering words or ideas that promised to be solutions to "getting things done" – all of them obvious solutions – *practical solutions* (unlike those of her "very dear brother's") – which she'd offer to me and Angus as a way of being able to "solve" the way that we were living, which was always going badly (according to her). This *solving* being definitely a family thing. A family obsession. And so how she would be discovering, constantly – inevitably – new and "highly progressive" ideas to help us address all of our problems with "getting around to doing" what we needed to do. Yes, even my perversity – my "extraordinary perversity", as I heard her once say about me to mum. Not using the same sorts of ideas as dad of course – never obscure ideas that no one but "maddies" had ever heard of, but the sorts of words or ideas that had become the same that everyone was using – everyone who talked on radio. Everyone on television. And so, thinking about how this simple word "mindful" might be applied to me, to my situation: that instead of standing here at this door and becoming overwhelmed and sickened – becoming agonised with my sickening – I might, instead, have been doing something useful for everyone by "trying to be mindful" about it or, as Arijit once described it to me, recognising *what could be done simply by accepting my thoughts and feelings.* And so "centring" myself in such a way that I would be "in a much better state of mind". Paying attention to the muscles in my body – of course the *right* bits of muscle – one after the other. *As everyone else in the world seems to manage to do it*, my auntie B would have added very quickly if she'd been watching or listening, and so breaking the spell of its seductive and useful effects – the magic of the *mindfulness mantra* – with her impatience to get going in me something more immediately productive. So that I didn't "waste any more time" avoiding the one specific thing that she had long been anxious for me to do *if I wasn't going to end up like her brother* (as she used to say). Yes, this so very ordinary situation with the muscles and the necessity to use or at least notice them, as she would have learned from the radio too. So very easy to address, as she had also heard (perhaps). And that there were so many courses you could do – so many of them free. This way all of our problems could become, after sessions like these, nothing but meaningless problems – *redundant problems*, I was thinking, even though – at the very same time – I also knew that I wasn't being fair to auntie B, since she had always wanted "the best" for us. Had tried to "listen". Was always "listening" to us, except in that year when it all fell apart. And so even now I could see that without this technique of *mindful* living – without such calming and *mindful awareness* – the harder I'd be working to do what I needed to do with the house – to clear it out – an enormous effort, as it still seemed to me, and one so completely against the odds. That in fact I might only be putting this enormous effort, with my *mind-chasing* habit of thinking – my unbearably *cluttered way of thinking* – my so very *unhelpful* way of thinking – all this *mindless* thinking – into doing the reverse. Even you, Teun, you would never say "mindless". Never quite such goading words as "mindless". Instead you would be "amazed", as you say, at how very "irrational" I can be. Regularly you describe how extraordinarily surprised you are when, after seeming to agree to do the one thing that "we discussed", I then carry on as if I had never taken in a single aspect of the matter that we'd supposedly agreed on during that earlier, supposed discussion. As if the whole time of our supposed discussion (when I was apparently nodding and even speaking – "agreeing"), some strange, sabotaging part of myself was working hard *against* that nodding – *against* that speaking, and so *against* the content of those words of agreement that I must have allowed myself to say. Of course, I don't intend to do this, Teun. Please believe me when I say I don't have the least memory of all this fakery. And yet I know that this happens because there have always been those slippages between one thing and another. Because even as I start to do one thing – say, to walk to the shops to buy us some milk – I have a sense that what I'm doing – this walking – this intention to buy – is the very thing that I *shouldn't* be doing. That in fact there is something *else* I should be doing *before* this buying of the milk – something else that is more important. *Far more important.* And of course, I will never be able to think of that necessary, important thing or problem that is waiting for me to notice it, even though I will also get a sense of it being something simple like a bill that, in falling overdue, would already be running to thousands of pounds. Or the person I had once promised to visit, who for long slow hours – even days or months – has been waiting patiently for me to arrive – one of those fragile people who didn't want to remind me of my commitment, and who sits there motionless in the dark watching the clock – so definite had I been about my intentions when I rang this person to promise I would come. So clear, so specific. *I'll see you on Tuesday, at eleven.* And so even as it might seem that I have *at last* decided to do the one thing that would help the two of us in practical terms (say, to replace the microwave oven that hasn't been working for years), my mind is already pressing down hard to counter that thought – braking on it – slowly at first and then sharply – and after pulling the thought in towards the oil-hot centre of the machinery inside me – perhaps my *mindful interior* – that perfectly "centred", pink-upholstered interior just for a moment – this same mind then niftily moves the gears so that I move with the whole of my weight, the whole of my person, precisely and decisively the *other* way around.

This dread I have of being the one who is still holding the lever that, once pulled, will change everything around her, destroying it all. Doing it *unwittingly.* The one who will cause a building, an entire world, to fall in on itself, *unwittingly.* The one who is discovered on the very wrong side of an action, still holding that lever, and who hasn't tried to stop the action, or at least tried to slow it down, so that the precious remnant – with all of its detail and history – this everything-piece-of-something that is about to be crushed, destroyed – with no chance of being reassembled or preserved or remembered – might not yet be entirely and forever lost to the world. Perhaps this was why the Song Dong treatment of the house had seemed so promising, Teun. At least at the beginning. How excited I had been – so very excited and relieved, too, to have something, you must have noticed – when I explained to you "everything" the evening I left for Australia. Relieved not simply to offer my one-time art school mentor, Nathaniel Lord, who had once believed in me *against the odds* – which is to say against the sceptics at art school – but also as a way to parry the commitment he had hoped to get from me about the Wall of "Still Lives" that had "piqued" his interest, as he said, as soon as I mentioned it – the one "fascinating" part of what I was doing or at least supposedly doing that had made him "so curious", as he kept on saying to me as well. Relieved that I could turn out such a magnificent display of wit and thought for Nathaniel Lord, but also for myself by way of making sense, in some much more graduated, system-atic manner, of the unbearable horror of everything I had been left with here in the family house. Of course, at the time of running into Nathaniel Lord at the opening of that group show in Hackney before I left for Australia, dad had just died and the house and its contents were not yet the main thing on my mind. I'd been thinking about dad at the time, I'm pretty sure – the shock and the guilt that came with the news of his illness and death. Primarily the guilt. Dad, and not the house, since it was the joke of that exhibition in Hackney that was taking up so much of my thoughts – that supposedly "*cutting-edge* exhibition", as you kept on calling it, where my pieces had been shoved right to the furthest and most emptied-out corner of the space – jammed at the back near the toilets and the table of drinks, don't forget. So handy, in fact, to the toilets. You might remember that I said, at the time, that if I had known how bad things had got to – meaning with dad, of course, even though I probably also meant this situation with the show and the gallery owners who had been messing me around – whom I couldn't bear to talk to in the way I probably needed to – telling you that if I could have predicted how bad it would be, I would have left for Australia a lot, lot earlier. Left to go back while I still had a chance to see dad before he died. But when you had asked me how I would have known just when it was bad enough, I hadn't been able to answer you, since my thoughts had already moved from dad onto my work and my inclusion in the show – the ongoing problem with the treatment of my work in such "eclectic contexts as these", where, of course, my pieces hadn't sold in the first half-hour of the opening, as others' had done. My pieces conspicuously lacking that bright red dot in a room where the walls were otherwise breaking out with them everywhere. The *usual rash of sycophancy and ignorance* (as I was going on about later that night to you in the car). And so I'm saying to you now, here, that I hadn't been able to answer you then because, in both cases, it was too hard to know. Since there had been a kind of doubling of the situation of dad – and hence my family – with myself and my work – this sliding between one and the other that was complete and convincing. Since I could see – even then – that there had never been a time that wasn't bad or bad enough, because of course when I left the country that first time it was bad – bad with my family at least, as you have so often said yourself. And yet also bad the whole time that we children were young and not making sense of our worlds in any kind of way. Bad when I developed anorexia, or just bad before the chill capabilities of anorexia made my world so orderly, so quiet, so definite, so secure. Bad when I decided to stop this tendency to self-starve – forcing myself to stop it short once I saw what I was doing to Angus who was copying what I did, starving himself too, "fading away", as I heard – his bird-winged shoulders, the hollows over his jaw, his grim, set mouth. Bad that I'd had to give it up fast, then – incredibly fast, but slowly too – if only to save Angus, because there was nothing else that could help me then. Nothing at all. Bad when I moved out, suddenly, "on a whim", as auntie Beryl and even mum had put it at the time, and into what I had told them was "just a student household" – this moving out that had promised to solve (for me) my problems with living, since, after all, hadn't I moved out to share with "a couple of like minds", as I had put it to you once – Eileen and Sonya – people I "felt entirely comfortable around"? People from art school whom I could talk to at any hour of the day or night, and for as long as I liked? Them and me – all of us talking in long and tremendous, unrestrained detail about all of our particular interests, and at any time that worked for us – long conversations, and constant, about everything we wanted to talk about – talking, always talking. Sleeping and talking. No need to resist this basic desire to live in the way we preferred, which meant allowing ourselves this switching, at random, between talking at all hours of the day and night, drunk or sober, and then shutting our doors so we could stay alone in our emptied-out heads. This moving out and away from the confusions of the family house in Chatswood, which should indeed have shifted my world into a far better order – indeed into a perfect order, as it seemed to do at the time since only then did my periods return – this reordering process that had seemed to happen so easily, and apparently painlessly, too. And yet, as I know I have told you many times before – boring you on so many occasions – my situation in this supposedly ideal way of living had degenerated, within months, into that scourge of loneliness and anxiety and paranoia, which is to say into that weirdly competitive situation with my art school friends. Because even from the beginning, I had become confused about the never-stated tendencies to anorexia that had drawn us together into our obsessive talking and "sharing" – all of our "sharing" – about the meaning of existence and the "right way" of doing things. This anorexia that it had become impossible, strangely, ever to discuss. And my artwork too, which – as I could see – had been freezing up, becoming all the more stilted the more we talked about *the role of art in this society that we were forced to live in*. Bad, then, but bad that it had also seemed I was always on the brink of doing something brilliant – something that would become full and palpable and brimming – always about to tip, to spill, to colour the world into the tones and spectrums I couldn't yet see but knew, nonetheless, I would recognise the instant it poured itself forth. Yes, the feeling of it moving unseen inside me, and about to become real – always about to become visible and real. All this promise, indeed, welling up inside me *despite* nothing ever managing to colour the world, let alone brimming. This way, too, that I was also trying, or at least intending "sometime soon", to make my artwork consistent with the world I could see in my head, and which we three had envisaged together (Son and Eileen and I). Always consistent. Always working hard to be clear and "well-thought-out" and, of course, *meaningful*. This sense that *all* we needed, at the time, was the guts, the patience, the determination to make it happen through our "aesthetic practices". And so the shock at home, in my family, with Leah. The terrible silence. No one wanting to talk or to stir our pain. It being better to keep away from it all. And then the August flood – that precipitous welling from the drains – those rains in Camperdown – those rains in Sydney. That putrid and lumpy grey mud that rose like a giant slug from the metal grill at the bottom of our street and so ruined everything we had left on the floor on the ground level of the house. Everything first ruined by the water and the mud and soon definitely ruined by the memory of that flooding – the ruining that went on long, long, and long after we had finished with the scraping and the cleaning, even long after we had moved into different houses – cities – countries. That constant anxiety about what the others were thinking about what had happened – the unevenness of the damage. The *flooding damage*. Since of course everything that Sonya had made for her assessments at art school had been destroyed. Everything of hers, but only some of mine. Not much of Eileen's. "The least of it" mine. And so with this, the slow but growing conviction that I was certainly "in the wrong" – that I had done something irrecoverable by having lost so little, by "nabbing" the upstairs front bedroom for myself, as I had supposedly done, although neither of them ever said it quite like that in my hearing. I just *knew* they thought it. But then there was nothing I could do to tip our existence back into the old equilibrium of easy talking – that, in fact, the more I tried to redress what I could, the more they despised what I said and what I did. None of it tolerated. There being no grounds for what

I was saying, apparently. And so the whole of what had once flowed so easily between us – none of it belonging to one or the other of us particularly – all of that gone and destroyed by the rains and the flood. Bad and bad, since hadn't I betrayed them as well – *and on top of it all* – hadn't I "run off to the teachers" with that performance idea about bodies and food, the idea we'd come up with together, as I'd thought, so soon after the flooding? This way that, by pushing myself to speak like this *so publicly* – and on *their behalf* – I might make amends? Bad that I had done this in the first place, as it seemed "so obviously" – and yet bad, too, that I was slow to include them in the official discussions about *their idea*, as they went on to call it. This idea I thought we had agreed to run with together but in which I was to be granted no "material part": this one about "the horror of the family meal" – its essential horror – that we'd joked about "socking to the art school" in all of its "awkward ugliness", with all of *our* awkward ugliness as well. With this image of this socking, this assault, that was not actually to be ours in origin but something that would come from the disgust of the meals. This constant assault, as we saw it, whenever we tried to pick apart what it was that was so awkward about the mealtimes as we remembered them at home – what we "really couldn't bear". Yes, the passivity and horror of our situation, as I still remember describing what we were "imagining doing" to Nathaniel Lord, my then art history teacher at art school. This situation where, as I'd explained it, "all we had" was our bodies, our refusals, to push between our beings and the "colonising intentions" of others – their "so awful concern" (I remember saying) – their horrendous miming of "only *seeming* to care". Their "dripping dank love", as one of us had called it (was it Eileen?). This continual bombardment of disgusting substances, where it was always *our* bodies and *our* minds that were not being allowed to be anything more than some sort of voiding vessel for *them* – for others. A kind of "*vomitous* vessel" (Sonya). And so this pitching of the idea of the "happening" to one of the teachers at art school (as I thought I was doing) – this "wonderfully *baroque* and fascinating idea", as Nathaniel Lord had actually called it when he heard me out. How he had smiled "that goofy smile", I then made sure to tell Sonya and Eileen as soon as I got home that day. How perfect his response. How keen. Fired up. And yet they were appalled – appalled, shocked – that I had broached it *like this*. Their: "Why did you tell him? Who gave you the right?" Yes, bad that I had done this – bad I had said this – but bad, too, that there hadn't been a reason I could give in my defence. Bad that I was weak, very obviously – that I lacked any plan, any clear comprehension of what it was that I thought I was passing on between them and him. Bad, what's more, that I was always "giving in to other people" (Sonya). Always losing hold of what was most important, apparently. Always too easily letting go of what I should, rather, be keeping whole – entire, distinct, and ours (*theirs*). And so how wanton I felt then. Bad and bad. Clearly *I must have had a reason to do what I had done*. Everything I do is wanton, I was then convinced – I never seem to have a reason for anything I do or even plan to do. And yet, bad that it was also impossible to tell them (Eileen and Sonya) that I was actually proud that Nathaniel Lord hadn't managed to get me to admit to our anorexia – our *shared history of anorexia* – this anorexia that, as he had seemed so clearly to suspect (or so I thought at the time), had "brought us together" at art school. Do you remember me saying this once, Teun? This anorexia that (as I'd got the feeling) Nathaniel Lord would have wanted to know more about if only he could. How persistent he had been about "the family meal" we were supposed to be alluding to in this artwork – the disgust of the family meal, which, suddenly, I knew I could not possibly account for in any way that would make sense to him. How he had pressed me to explain what it was about the "disgust" that we were wanting to "stage", as he put it, "in such a bold and astonishingly naïve way". Surely it was just food and love and care, he said. Just food going bad. Food going off. Was that "care going off", "care becoming dead"? "And all of you *sisters* in this?" he had asked with such an insinuating smile, an insinuating look. Hence my elaborate attempts to come up with something much more reasonable, much more acceptable, for why we were doing this – something that might convince someone as discerning (I'd thought) as Nathaniel Lord. Hence that account of the "abject situation of being women in our society". Abject as women, I'd said, from a patriarchal point of view. Yes, the way – the "continual way" that we – women – were always being subjected to the refuse of the world – "the most abject of refuse" (as I had said). The confusion of matter that needed to be understood as "nice" or "good" from one perspective, and which could also be understood as wrong, sick (thus the food being *off*). And so the "incursions of ordinary, everyday horror from a feminist perspective", as Nathaniel Lord had then described it for me when he seemed to *get* what I was trying to make him swallow. Yes, this apparent giving in to what had seemed, at the time, to be the so fashionable and yet also so entirely relevant and convincing way to *see it all*. Relevant of course – entirely relevant – but also way off course from what it was that we had been thinking then, if we had ever been able to name what that particular something was. This way that our bodies – our actual and horrible bodies – these bodies that we really didn't like too much – that we really didn't know what to do with – which burdened us with questions and problems from one hour to the next – how these same bodies had become stand-ins for the much broader, more acceptable notions that were easier to describe because others had already described them for us. In other words, stand-ins for the more "hard-hitting" statements about "women" and "patriarchy" and "culture", as Lord had kept putting it – the "sullying patriarchal gaze of the projector", as we ended up writing in our statement for our assessment, which had now become a stand-in for what we had then called the "sullying patriarchal gaze of the viewer". And so nothing about what *we* might have been performing if *we* had been able to understand any more about what it was that we were trying to say. Nothing but what Sonya (later) saw as, clearly, the "titillating value" of our skin, our "folds". Our "boldness", as Nathaniel Lord had called it. And so nothing about our relatively awful-looking, still wrinkled-at-the-elbow sort of emaciation at the time, which he might well have considered to be nothing more than evidence of a more ordinary-looking emaciation now that I had thrown him off the scent – the very ordinary-looking emaciation, as I would expect he was thinking, of many young women of our age and times. So, yes, bad then that I had been so "susceptible to our gracious Lord's perverted idea for the three of us", as Sonya has put it only recently somewhere. And bad because I had turned out to be pathetically susceptible to *artspeak*, too. How susceptible I had been, as well, to the "promises of institutionalised vampirism", as I read in one of Sonya's more recent rants on Facebook – susceptible to the supposed "charisma of someone who only gets his rocks off by feeding on others" – and especially the "weirdness" of others, if "they can suit his designs", when, or indeed if they "toe the line" – always trying to make himself appear in the very right places, "the very right shitheap", as Son so elegantly put it and continues to put it out about Nathaniel Lord in her Instagram or Facebook feeds. These traces of her peculiar feud that I should not be able to see anymore since the time she *un*friended me after my visit to Casino, and yet which I still continue to see all the same, since she tags me in among so many others, and of course via Eileen who *shares* it all. And yes, bad that I was weak, so "transparent to a predator" as "our Lord and Master" is supposed to be. And yet bad, too, that instead of dropping the idea of the food and bodies "happening" at once, as I might have done the minute I realised the awfulness of what I had got into for Eileen and Son, I had "gone on doggedly ahead with it", pushing myself to do what I had said I wouldn't – which is to say, to "betray" our tentative thoughts. To betray my friends, as Sonya still apparently sees what I did all those years ago. Bad, because instead of doing what was necessary to "keep ownership" of our idea that had now become *his*, I had "pigheadedly" gone ahead with "forcing" them (apparently) to get involved in something that they *had* to do as well if they didn't want to fail the year. Yes, bad then, but also bad when the three of us managed – in fact – to do well with the piece. All high distinctions. What more to say? And yet bad just to think how it was with us at the time, because how awful *I* – at least – must have looked as I perched on that child-sized wooden chair beside them on the pallet – naked, of course – half cold, half hot under the lights in the dark of that automatic slide show that Eileen had rigged for us with "our gracious Lord's *personal* carousel", as Sonya still calls that yellow-cream cube from which he would project for the class those Rubens and Titian nudes. So entirely exposed. Such a specimen of awfulness – since *I* was the only one, as it felt at the time, that was transparent – and transparent in a pathetic and blood-less way – to everyone there – the whole of my abject need to fit in with the others – with Lord, with Eileen, with Sonya – completely on show. And so my clear inability to marry my thoughts and feelings with my actions, as I knew Sonya especially could sense. Or even Eileen, who had closed her eyes and was so easily able to *will*. Her "perfectly hewn" sense of becoming nothing but an "object" (Lord). As something that had already "gone dead under the lights" (Son). Sonya who had glared right back at anyone who looked at us during the performance – glaring, too – of course – at me. Her challenge becoming the centre of the quote-unquote theoretical and aesthetic challenge of the piece. My continual unease. My undecidedness about how to be, as a body or even as a thinking self, in that piece. Bad, then, that for a long time after this, I was obsessed with doing everything possible to assuage the feelings of my friends Eileen and Sonya – everything I could do to make things better. This necessary assuaging. Everything in my ongoing attempts to guess long ahead about how they might *take* a thought I wanted to tell them, but never succeeding in getting close to resolving what I figured I had to resolve with either of them, at least with Son (this abject wish that it might be possible to start our friendship again from a smooth and definite zero). But bad, too, when I was driven, as it seemed, to keep away from them – from everyone I knew – as far as I could from this house, as well, and the people in it. The country as a whole. The obligatory visits, okay – but otherwise the need – the desperate need – to keep to the other and outer edge of the earth. And so, bad when I heard that Angus had gone into rehab and I hadn't even noticed he was going this way with the ekkies and hash he had been using since high school. Bad when he found religion and his face had drained of everything I recognised. Bad when, after years of never getting round to saying what I meant to say to her – always avoiding it – never putting words to what it was that I might have said if I'd known what to say – bad when my mother died from that stroke in the refuse of the house. Bad when dad was continuing to live on his own in the increasing chaos and befuddlement of his ideas and determinations – although more to the point, bad that I couldn't bear to think about this in any way at all. Bad, too, when Angus moved in with him, although perhaps it was good. Bad, quite definitely, when Angus was lying to me about not coping (and hence bad that I wouldn't have wanted to hear he wasn't coping). Bad, since every day of my life has always felt tenuous to me – always about to be destroyed by a reversal, an unsettling – even in an instant – destroyed, as it would always seem to be by the weight and the force of everything that, until this coming moment of shocked awareness, I had forgotten or ignored. The sludge of it pushing against me. And so the need to resist such a pushing if I wanted to remain whole and entire – to enact, with force, what could only be a countering pressure. Hence those appalling and very *willed* phone calls to dad after mum had died. Do you remember, Teun? When it was my self-imposed ritual to make that call to dad as often as I could. Always on a Tuesday and early in the morning, as you will probably recall if you think about it even for a second. This feeling that it was necessary for me to do this – that I *had* to do this. This necessity to ring "on a regular basis" – to make sure that dad was "okay" – just to check that dad was eating anything other than his usual extreme concoctions, which might only be organic eggs and "kelp", for instance, or only the wheat grains that he had sprouted in an "esky" with the help of a light bulb in the bath, as Angus had discovered one day when he arrived home after a week away "starving", as he described it afterwards, and hoped to find something in the fridge – anything other than those ten-year-old jars of jam and condiments that mum had bought and dad never used. This feeling that I should really be cutting short my own existence in order to give all of my attention and energy to *dad's* existence – a feeling that I have always lived with and have either been consciously or unconsciously resisting the whole of my life – that I really *should be there* for dad, as well as for mum and Angus, and so always prepared to be given over and so swamped by his (and their) existence in place of my own. This sense that I usually do nothing but fore-stall a necessary succumbing to what is inevitable and necessary and moral – in other words, what I have always felt to be a sudden and imminent succumbing to the massive force of their *obviously overriding needs*. And so also knowing that, in such a predicament, I might be able to resist the hints, but not the request. Never the overt request. That it would not be possible to refuse dad or mum if a request came in. And yet the request *never came*, I only realised, then, in the hallway in Chatswood on the day that the first of the skips was arriving – realising how I have always been dreading the request – the bald, objective request, rather than one that was only manip-ulative and wheedling. The direct request, rather than one that was hinted at. Yes, indeed, this request had never come – not from mum, not from Angus, not from dad. No, never. Not even in the end, from an ailing dad. Just that surge of warmth between us when he heard that it was me on the phone – a surge that moved in an instant outwards and towards me – a yellowish flame – into the first small flaring of "ideas" that he wanted to tell me about: the state of the world and what was "necessary" for *us all to do*. Perhaps something about our need to understand how the volcanic contributions to worldwide CO_2 were greater than the human contribu-tions, or the need to employ "the military" to plant out the desert in Australia with a mathematically efficient arrangement of trees. His way of continu-ally dismissing the recommendations of the climate change scientists who "ignored all the evidence", as he put it – that "bunch of ratbags", as he also called "the lot of them". The evidence that he would enumerate in aston-ishingly precise and obsessive detail, but about which I have never been able to retain a single fact, a single supposedly reasoned line. And so this way I have never been able to respond to him in a rational manner because, rather than being able to listen or react with logic to what he was saying, I would always be putting all of my effort into making it *sound* as if I had been listening. Never actually listening but only *sounding* as if I were listening to the fiery run of his thoughts – those thoughts that soon were flaring fast, even raging, against "the medical profession" or "the climate change fanatics".

Seeming to listen so that these hot white thoughts wouldn't rage against *me* as well. And as you would know, now, from the kinds of stories I have told you over the years: if *you* had been the one that had grown up in these sorts of listening situations, *you* would have found that you wouldn't even have known in your body *how* to listen – and not only to rants whose factual sources were usually the most obscure and discredited – that is, to the sorts of rants that rose like naturally emanating fumes from the rash assertions and supposed data that can be found in articles sponsored by dubious supplement companies that someone like dad would have found in his local health food shop catalogue or a book discarded in a garage sale – not only to these sorts of rants, but also to anything – absolutely anything at all. Yes, never at all listening in a "normal way" to any kind of thing whatsoever, no matter how clear, how solid the thing was from an outsider's perspective. And so not even to talks by teachers. Group conversations. Lectures at art school. Because right in the moment that you realised you *should* be listening "properly" to something, you would also be realising that you had, already – earlier – stopped yourself from listening, and that your very realisation that you had stopped yourself from listening minutes, hours, days ago, made it all the more difficult to start again, to listen to somebody or something else, even from the point when you realised what had been happening to you with all this listening – when it wasn't yet too late, that is, to catch up with the thing. And you would be realising too – if you thought about it even for a second – that in all the years that you were growing up in this house in Chatswood, you'd *had* to stop listening. There having been so much at stake in *not* listening. So much to be destroyed by listening. Because you knew that if you listened for real – that is, properly, and with *appropriate attention* – to the rants that someone like my father was always coming out with, you would soon be overwhelmed by the sheer quantity of what had to be listened to. Of what *demanded* to be listened to – with the very least of it, odd, contentious, and usually wrong, entirely skewed – with the worst, a deluge of catastrophe and threat that could press you into a panic that would drive you over the edge of something that you couldn't yet see but knew was there. From a sheer instinct to survive, you would have learned that it was vital to put all of your strength and determination into only *seeming* to listen to the interminable and often terrifying monologues that you had never in your entire life been able to bear. Years and years and decades of not listening – of protecting yourself from rants that usually drew you into a vortex of rage (his). You might remember, then, how relieved I was when I heard that Angus had moved in with dad so that he, Angus, could save on costs and "keep an eye" on him. Yes, thinking about all this again at the house when I stepped off the porch to use the side of my foot to push the bag of rubbish that was starting to irritate me by the way it was leaning so loosely and helplessly there – to push the bag, and then the wires and the boxes, clear of the path – in fact kicking them away from the concreted squares and onto the tussocks of half-dead grass. The idea of Angus moving in here being such a godsend at the time. The promise that, at least, there was somebody in the place of the apparently willing and interested listener that my father needed – a somebody that wasn't and couldn't be me. And yet Angus can't have coped, I was thinking in this moment when, after kicking, too, at the bags of liquids and bottles I had left on the porch – pushing them away from where I was working, so there would be greater scope – a greater clearance – for this *necessary work*, I then crossed the lawn to the driveway, my attention having been caught by the old ironwork gate at the entrance to the footpath, whose modernist loops and bars had been one of my earliest fascinations. Years of staring out at this pair of gates from the window of the lounge room – their symmetrical spirals, top and bottom – the simplicity of the spirals – the parallel bars of iron between the spirals – the whole of it rusting through the yellowish-white of the paint. Most of it rust. And so with me now splitting the gates at the middle and starting to pull the two halves back and inwards as far as I could to clear the driveway. The difficulty of getting the closest one open and so over the garden bed, past the edge of the concrete. The thought that I should even be skewering the dead grey soil between the aloes with the bolt that I was trying to drag across the concrete slabs so that the skip would be closer to the house when it arrived – so that this whole business with the house could be done as quickly and as simply as possible. And so: Angus, I was thinking, because I knew – and had to face – that Angus had been unable to cope with dad. That Angus must have had even *less* tolerance than I had for dad's "ideas", as he called them – it not being possible, he used to say, to be in the same room as dad and those "crazy ideas". But at least *he would have been there for dad*, I was telling myself when I knocked the heads off the smaller aloes as I scraped and scraped the gate even further over the garden bed. Ruthless with the aloes that mum used to hate, as I remembered. Their dull-looking spread. These awful specimens that dad had rescued from the garden at his mother's place, apparently, when the block had been sold. But still, as I was pulling at the gates, I couldn't help remembering the time I told you about being worried and in fact even *troubled* about dad and Angus and everything that was happening with them here in Sydney – or should I say, beginning to tell you and then quickly adjusting what I was saying. Trying to change it, so that the implications of what I was saying about the "appalling" situation were not so clear – neither to you and nor to me. Because the way it struck me then, even as I was saying all this to you at the time, was that if I were *really* as worried and troubled as I was making out, I would *have* to be doing a lot more than I was doing at the time – so much more than those negligible (although still intolerable) calls on Tuesdays. The logic of it obvious (how it had seemed to me then). And hence my thought that there was no point at all in continuing what I was saying if I had no intention of doing anything different about the situation with dad – if I could not bear to do a thing about it. Because even to admit to the smallest of my concerns would also be to admit that I really should have *already* arranged things so that I'd *already* be back here in this house, in Australia, instead of over there with you in London. That I would *already* be back "with the family" – taken over by "the family". Taken over by *his* existence, in fact. Dad's existence. And so how it suited me *not* to think about how Angus was "usually rude", as I called it, to dad – that, unlike what I usually did with my habit of not listening, Angus

45

would criticise, constantly, even the very least – the most irrelevant – of something he (dad) had said. He (Angus) would dare, as I had never dared, to get up in the middle of one of dad's long explications of those supposedly new but always very worn and ever more complicated theories on natural gas and Radon, or the connection between the "British nation" and the lost tribes of Israel, or the causes of cancer and some sort of "bright light therapy" that "shrivelled up" all of the pathogens in our bodies. Angus getting up and walking away in such a manner and outburst of never-suppressed irritation that dad would shout out after him – complaining, rightly perhaps, that he (Angus) was *ridiculing his ideas*. Yes, the way that it so suited me to believe that Angus's sudden eruptions and his walkings-away were actually good for dad, or at least for Angus. The way I would believe that at least this sort of reaction – that is to say, Angus's reaction – would have been effective in stopping those interminable lectures that the two of us had heard over and over, the whole of our lives. In fact, I remember saying how *glad* I was that Angus was able to manage what I could never manage – that it was, indeed, to his credit that he (Angus) was capable of putting a much more honest and effective end to any expectations from dad that he, the son – the expected listener – was listening to him (the father) anymore. And yet, you might remember that, despite all of this – this apparent solving of the situation with dad and his lecturing – I had seen that the house had nonetheless turned into even more of an overwhelming state when I travelled back to Australia again, to see dad and Angus after mum had died – which is to say, just seven months on. This was something that I could not yet admit to you, Teun. After all, when *hadn't* the house been like this in all the years I had been alive? At least it wasn't Angus's house that was oozing and splitting with the accumulation of decades, I was saying then, at least to myself – only *dad's house*. Angus had his own house in Stanmore, as you probably remember, since mum had thought to leave him the house she had bought with her inheritance from that uncle Pete, and far from being envious of Angus that *he* was left with that house, I have always been glad that she'd left it to Angus. Haven't

I always said this? Glad, perhaps, because in *this* way it was easier not to resent this brother of mine for his part in facing me with what I should have been doing myself for dad if I were the kind of daughter I thought I ought to be. Okay, some faint bitterness that mum hadn't thought of me in her will, or rather how she had clearly resented that I'd kept away from her on the other side of the world – how she had planned what she did with the Stanmore house as a kind of punishment. The niggling awareness that for these many long years she should have planned this coup against me – this effective coup – and hence I was bitter and guilty, but also glad. Glad to be forced into such a position that I couldn't resent Angus but instead had to be glad he was doing what he was doing in looking after dad. Because it wasn't as if his whole world had collapsed into dad's, I remember explaining to you when I'd got back to England after that particular visit. This necessity to say such a thing to you – to anyone – because, of course, his world *had* collapsed into dad's world. Completely collapsed. Always this centripetal force – this centripetal force as well as its opposite, the centrifugal force, I was thinking there on the driveway. These two forces that had existed for us in that house – these unbearable forces that cannot co-exist. Because I have always known that mum's world had collapsed into dad's world the moment she married him – a sudden collapse, if also a gradual and continual dissolution of her existence, as it seemed to me too, whenever I attempted to think about what had happened to her over the years – the worsening of the house – the worsening of everything that kept her distinct and alive. The loss of determination to earn her own income anymore. The loss of any separate sort of existence that wasn't just an act of resistance. The strength of her resistance to a husband who could become so very angry suddenly – and even violent. So often violent (and a violence that is still hard for me to remember as anything more than muted bursts of nothingness – blank – a startled sense of the walls or pieces of furniture in a room). And hence a necessary resistance, I might have said to you then. A *dogged resistance*. But, yes, that definite collapse, as I also remembered while I was pulling and scraping at the aloes – those ugly aloes – and once again now as I write up these notes for you in this document that I will send you in time for you to read before I arrive back in London – so that you might see what I am trying to get at here. So you might begin to understand why it is all so difficult for me to put into spoken words. That complete collapse, even though I also have to acknowledge that from *her* perspective – at least from her perspective as I imagine it now – it has often seemed that, in marrying dad and moving to Sydney, her world had expanded to an infinite degree. Because you have to remember that she had travelled down from Brisbane for this marriage to dad – from "stifling" Brisbane, as she used to call it – this "stifling" being a word that had confused me, because the only time we went there we had shivered in the wooden house that belonged to her uncle as we listened to the rattling glass in their louvred frames. The persistent and leaking cold that I remember from that visit. Becoming restless in the room he had put the three of us children in. Everything wooden and sheened, almost wet with the chill. And that strange sort of uncle – our *great-uncle Pete*, as he was supposed to be, even though not at all an uncle by blood, as she sort of explained. And neither very old. This uncle Pete who had always wanted – and even assumed (I'd learned), since her parents were dead – my mother's "involvement" in the printing business he ran only three streets away – this "family business", as he termed it to us, because it was her right, her obligation, her curse, even though the family had not *quite* been the family she was part of – a sort of family connection that mum never explained, and which it is obviously far too late for me to find out anything more about. But if the world had expanded for mum when she had run away from that uncle and his dreary fate for her (that is, overseeing the printing of so many annual calendars for other small and chilly and perhaps stifling businesses in Brisbane) – running away, what's more, to the "big bad south", as uncle Pete had called it, where the breadth of "your father's interests", as mum liked to call them on occasions, had saved her – she might well have got a lot more than she hoped to get. That prim sort of emphasis she would use when describing dad's "interests" – his so obviously "wide-ranging interests", his *peculiar* interests" – not stifling at all, perhaps, but only fierce and strange. These careening obsessions of dad's like the wildest tracings of a very free mind. Indeed, whatever had happened in terms of expansion when mum had met dad, it is likely that she was soon swept along by these streams of thought and their wild, wild tracings – perhaps even buoyed along for a while. How extraordinary it must have been at the time. But then instead of becoming loosened too, mum had been overwhelmed – clearly overwhelmed – as the whole of her existence merged with the wildness and strangeness, which is to say, each of her preferences merging – her myriad capabilities – whose possibilities I once got a sense of when, some years ago, I went into that room next to the laundry that dad didn't touch. That room she had used for "getting the tax together", as she put it (the books, and the clippings – those innumerable newspaper clippings about all sorts of subjects, most of them warnings about dangerous substances, dangerous practices). Every bit of these parts of her existence merging and so surrendering (at least initially) to dad's existence. All of it merging and drowning in the wake of dad's existence, with only the smallest and strongest of her points of resistance sticking up out of the swill – that is, only the bits that had always looked trivial and petty to me. Her criticisms, her complaints. Her aping, as I saw it, of what had always seemed to be the most boring lives of our neighbours in the vicinity in Chatswood. The very least of her quibblings and preferences sticking up like thin dark sticks in the swirling mud of it all. And yet even the smallest of these resistances, no doubt, giving her a way to survive – in fact, becoming essential to her survival as a separate being from my father, even though, very clearly – since not able to resist the stronger currents of *his* existence – these points, these sticks, would have soon been submerged as well. And so it only struck me as I kept pulling on the aloes – pulling the smaller and wizened ones out of that ditch of a garden by the driveway and doing everything I could, short of using my own sort of stick or spade, to gouge them out – its only striking me then that I had never been able to see any of this for what it was at the time: that is, as evidence of her essential resistance. Her *necessary resistance*. And so with Angus, too: his necessary resistance, as it also felt to me in that first and only visit to dad after mum had died – even when I could sense that Angus had started to merge with dad's existence, no matter that he, Angus, had kept on arguing against dad whenever he (dad) opened his mouth. Either taking small and petty issue with every one of dad's exaggerations that he (dad) had taken in holus-bolus from all the books that he read – the books, all those "peculiar books" and "peculiar magazines", as mum used to call them – anything at all that he (dad) had pulled into himself in the way he would have done from the internet too if he had been so much younger – from the incredible quantities of refuse that is lying all around us, wide and high on the web – and so Angus either picking apart the smallest aspect of anything dad said or rejecting it out of hand. Yes, Angus resisting, which is to say, taking issue with every single fact and statement that dad would come out with. First taking issue with him and then next (or instead) walking out on him – that is, cutting short his own immediate commerce with dad's many supposedly "*vital* theories for understanding the world", which would probably have included the Rife machine theory or the British-Israel theory. All of the numerous theories, one after the other, that never cohered into a single view or a single summation – never being *able* to cohere – since at any one time, it always seemed that we were supposed to understand that the theory he was regaling us with, in that moment, was the *only* theory worth listening to. That this single theory was the "only one" that "explained it all". At the time, though, when I heard the way that Angus used to argue against dad in the way that he did, I would find – if you remember, from my descriptions, Teun – that I couldn't bear to witness it a single minute longer. How excruciating it was – and no matter that he (Angus) was generally in the right, you could say, from a logical perspective. For Angus used to take issue with even the most trivial and least contentious of the statements dad would come out with from the point of view of fact and "logical connection" – saying to dad: "Like none of that makes sense", "none of it connects". Even jumping straight onto the sorts of minor-sounding points of exaggeration that dad would often make in the preliminaries to any one of his many ongoing "ideas", which is to say his universalising theories. Angus jumping straight onto the first small point in any slow-winding upwards of intense feeling that it had always seemed too dangerous (for me) to interfere with – cutting straight in at the coil, if you like. Yes, Angus's continual, almost unthinking, resistance to everything dad would say, and even before he was saying it. His essential resistance, perhaps. Because, as I think you need now to realise as well: without this resistance, without this fast cutting in on the coil of everything dad would say, the *whole* of his existence (that is, Angus's existence) would have been submerged in dad's. Because otherwise he *was* submerged. In every other aspect of their lives together he was submerged. Yes, even the way that Angus would sink in low, without a word or a complaint, into those endless re-runs of *M*A*S*H* that dad still expected to watch at the same time every evening. Angus always capitulating to dad and his tremendously childish need to keep watching this show every day of his life. The studio laughter that showered the room where they were sitting together staring at the pictures. "*Wonderful!*" dad would call out with a fierce ejaculation in the very same spots he had always called out, and for as long as I could remember: "*This is priceless! Somebody should be bottling and selling it!*" Yes, bad then, that by the time the ancient video tape from the collected series had clunked so easily into the machine and the music started rolling out – over the room, over the house – those expected little run of notes – the whole of Angus's existence had already begun to sink and mingle with dad's existence, which is to say, with the helplessness of our adolescence – Angus's existence – and mine too, that time I was there. The three of us becoming pulled so easily into that somnolent soup of an existence that, as *M*A*S*H* sent out its inevitable pat-a-pat sounds – its inevitable sequence of punchlines and laughter – soon became the best and the happiest of all possible existences that could ever occur in that Chatswood house.

And so: bad, as I could see it while I was still wrenching at those aloes from the horrible ditch beside the driveway. Bad, since, as it was occurring to me then: if I had been able to listen to dad as I should have been listening in those early few months after he had *lost his wife* – always listening carefully and in detail, and in such a *normal way*, as other people seem to be able to manage it with their parents – listening and responding instead of automatically *un*listening – if I had been able to do this, it is possible that I might have even been able to remain more active – and so far more alive – when I talked to him over the phone. Even on the trip out to see them both after mum had died, I might have been able to do or say something that succeeded in extricating us all from those re-runs of *M*A*S*H*. To say something that might have been adequate in responding to the peculiar text that Angus had sent me before dad collapsed, only weeks before he died. That startling admission that Angus had had enough.

This momentously confusing place. This running down of time, of things, of thoughts, of existence. This unbearably *entropic existence*, I was thinking as, with hands and arms now tingling from the scratches got from ripping out those splayed and vindictive plants by the driveway, I went back into the hall where I could see, in an instant, that there was a massive tarpaulin lying behind a pile of lightweight crates and plastic bags – a massive tarpaulin that I hadn't noticed before. And so you might think, as I realised in this instant when the hall seemed so different, suddenly – especially when the crates and the bags had been moved – you might think that so much of this problem I have been finding with the house is a problem of attitude, Teun. Yes, I am sure it is largely attitude. And so how easy it should have been then to "grab at this tarp", as we say it over here. *To tackle the problem of the tarp.* The "tarp" that was heavy, stiff with paint and, when pulled away from where it was pushed against the wall, gave out a deep sound – a deep and sucking, disgorging sound, as of something ripping, being pulled from its roots. My disgust rose in an instant, too, as, from out of the pores of the tarp, a scattering of what might have been flakes of paint or dust or wingless insects became airborne. And then once more, when I pulled the tarp further towards me and saw that there was a gap beneath: a waiting gap – a wide and fluffily smoothed-down place where the carpet looked pale and clean – soft and pale and seemingly moist. The horrendous softness of what *had* to have been the original carpet lying underneath, like somebody's sunless skin. And the thin turned legs of a writing desk that were pushing down deep into the plush – the walnut writing desk that might have been dropped from a precise moment in the past. Dropped from a height. This desk that had once held on its uppermost surface the only telephone in the house. The lot of it bare and mostly clean. And so how it hurt me to look at this section of pale cream carpet, and the pressed-in desk. I found myself pushing the tarp, then, back against the wall – my hands already pushing it, and with such determination, as if they, my hands, had separately decided that they were going to have to *deal with it another time*. But no, not just my hands. My hands were determined but the whole of me seemed to have decided as well. The sense, too, that surely there was something *else* that I needed to be doing *before* I got to this section of the hall, anyway. That the whole of this procedure of emptying out and readying the house was going the wrong way around – my approach to it flawed, and flawed in a fundamental manner.

And so you should be able to understand, now, the very thing that I have tried to describe to you lots of times before. This difficulty. This incredible difficulty. Because it's not just laziness that stops me, or perhaps not just laziness, since there is also the thingness of my resistance *to* what I am doing, which is also its own kind of active state. Think of it – yes, think of it in the same way, Teun, that I continue to create or fail to create my pieces – indeed, each of the pieces in this series "Still Lives" which, as you have conceded, requires the attention of a madman or perhaps mad*woman* to assemble. The details that obsess me. All the difficulties I have in maintaining the graduated view of the details through the layers of translucencies – by approaching it, perhaps, in the way that I do – by never planning ahead, since only ever playing with what happens in the moment of creating the thing – exploiting what happens – *what has already happened* – a high-wire terrifying way to go about it, as you have told me so often, when you've watched me, in the past. Why do I always approach it in the manner that I do when it would be *so much easier* to plan ahead – *to make a system* – to do it one bit at a time and then wait for the components to dry instead of "going on ahead", and so usually "from the wrong way around" (you observe)? Sketching out one thing and then "forcing the rest" to comply with what was only ever an accidental gesture – a happenstance mark? How do I endure it? Yes, the role of this resistance in what I do as I work. Always the resistance that drives me to force, to compress, to will into something as much as to avoid – and so, in the end, this bringing into everything I do "a very driven and *anal attention*", as you have called it, that wouldn't have been necessary if only I could have allowed "a measure of planning" to come in at the beginning of the process. First bringing all of my resistance and then – as if only to make up for the chaos, the stress – a desperate and seemingly mad drive to rescue those "only half-thought-about pieces" that you yourself would never have bothered with if *you'd* had the freedom from the office to pursue your own kinds of artistic projects. Yes, this very driven way of working, as well as that tendency of mine to ignore everything else in my life for the time that I am working on whatever I'm working on – and becoming anxious – churned. Tied into knots, by the inevitably tight-winding ways of my peculiar practice. We see the world differently, clearly, I remember saying that time when we had tried *going over the state of my studio together*, as you put it. The situation of my commitments, too, to the galleries that have been urging me to make this Wall that I have been writing and speaking about, even though I already have "more than enough" to contend with in this series I've been working on in the interim, as I have kept on saying as well. This series of "Still Lives" pieces. Individual pieces, or groups of threes and fours. This tendency to *over*commit – to *over*explain. As well as the clearly unliveable state of where I *allow myself to work*. And so it might or might not come as a surprise to you that, despite how it is when I'm definitely "onto something", it has not been enough that I have now been enlivened in every limb of my body to do this *clearing-out work* on this Chatswood house. This brutal work. So proud, actually, that I've been managing to do it – that I rang for the skip in the first place. Not enough that I have managed to *will* myself to work in a way that pushes hard and decisively against my usual instincts. Not enough, as even you should realise. Should recognise immediately. Because, as you also know, every time that I seem to have found the answer to something – some sort of solution – it usually turns out to be just another problem. Another obsession. Another way (as you would probably see it) of trying to avoid the unbearable sight that is revealed when you remove an old tarp(aulin) from its long-settled place in a hallway.

Of course, this has not been the only such moment of faltering in the course of "tackling the house". There have been plenty of moments like this in the process of clearing it out for the agents. Plenty of times when I have become helpless, suddenly, at the helplessness that is everywhere around me – these *signs* of helplessness, if you like. The helplessness of the carpet. The helplessness of the desk. The helplessness of myself, as well, since I have been continually overcome by a physical fear – a very physical disgust and loathing – when, if I wasn't just going to give in – to collapse and avoid – as I usually do with these sorts of pressures, I would have to push back hard against my own instincts – and so against this, my most basic reactions to "the demand of objects", as Nathaniel Lord might have put it to me if he were still scripting my by-lines: the fear – the horror – of contamination from even the least of these otherwise *anodyne* "objects". Which meant, yet again, forcing my hands to grab hold of that tarp – forcing myself to do this. To stay as blind as I could, and as unfeeling, too, to the rising disgust. To remain *brutally unfeeling*. Why is it, I was even thinking as I pulled for the second time on that tarp – why is it that I am made in such a way that I have to *continually force myself* to do what others can do so easily and without thinking at all? That I have to force myself against the horrendous vulnerability of what might only be a thing – an *object* – but might also be my father, as when he was dying alone, as I heard – and with nothing but the grey of the window in his room at the hospital – that rimless window that would have been starting to return something of the translucent edges of the bed and the wall and his drip apparatus back to him. This imagined end, but also the message that Angus had left on my phone about dad being dead and (apparently not yet twenty minutes after this) the message from Beryl's daughter Kate about me missing the funeral. "You *do* realise you missed it, don't you", this voice had said with its sweet and considerate thoughtfulness. As if this voice (call it Kate) had most wisely assumed that I had wanted to miss the funeral – and indeed *intended* to miss it – but thought that it was not such a nice thing to point out to me over the phone.

It was only then, as I forced myself to haul out the tarp – dragging it down the steps to the lawn, where it crouched as if still alive, as if it were about to spring – still deadly – now laughing at me from its surly folds – that I could see that my disgust at the not-so-disgusting – at the *opposite* of disgusting, as you have might have put it if *you* had been here to see that stretch of carpet I was still trying to avoid – the carpet and the desk that I had *so exposed* – that this response to the pathetic only, the vulnerable only, was quite a lot more difficult for me to cope with than anything else ahead of me in this house. Worse than the waves of foetid stink that assailed me each time I re-entered the hallway. The torpor of that stink. The slowing-down foulness of that stink. Worse than the flakings and the dust that had lodged in my membranes. In fact, all I could think of in this moment, then, were those flesh-coloured nighties my mother had got me to take – those overly limp nighties and those similarly pale singlets and A-line skirts, which she'd make me take back to London on the plane – "a few bags of things". All the useless crap, as I used to describe it when you asked me about them – none of them wanted of course, but none that I could toss out either. All of that discarded clothing of hers that still whiffed, somehow, of her hopes for me. Most of it never worn (since usually the wrong size, the wrong colour), but also some she had liked and even worn for a while, but somehow turned out not to be right for her – "too good to throw away". This clothing that, clearly, she couldn't bear to give to anyone else. That still smelled of this house – at least of *her part of this house* – and so of *her* in essence. So much of it shiny, smooth, and carefully kept. And then those clippings from the newspapers that even she, after everything she'd say about "other people's houses" – about other people's exemplary "orderliness and cleanliness", which needed to become *our* exemplary orderliness and cleanliness too. The clippings from those papers she evidently couldn't help amassing herself, since it took time, as she would say, to "go through" them all. Do you remember my horror, my gaping, at those Tetris-shaped pieces I was supposed to read and so take into myself and absorb – that, and all of the supposedly acceptable clothing? Hardly worn, as she continued to say. "Perfectly good". The smooth, flat sheen of the nylon skirts with their "practically invisible zippers" (only the faintest of yellowish stains at the edge of a hem perhaps – "nothing wrong with it", she used to say if I began to object – "*absolutely nothing*"). These and the clippings in their creased plastic sleeves with the remnants of Sellotape from other uses. The newspaper material itself not brittle yet, no matter that it might have been years she had kept them before pushing them into my hands. "Nothing wrong" with the substance of the clippings, if you like. And of course, it was "only information", as she would always put it if I objected to taking any of this onto the plane with me when I came. *All* I had to do was read the pieces and then throw them away, she'd say, and particularly the pieces of "information about Australia" that she knew I was far too busy to look out for by myself. Yes, I know you have noticed how these bags and bags have accumulated there in the corner of my studio. None of it touched again, obviously. All of it still in its white supermarket skins, and subdivided into sleeves or yet other, and smaller, plastic bags. These otherwise undifferentiated things – objects, *stuff* that I have only ever had the strength to remove from my suitcase and *not one inch further* from the place I've left them. But have you noticed, too, how I can never manage to throw any of it away? *How could I*, as I've always said to you. *I haven't even had a chance to look at it properly.* Yes, the arguments we've had over "all this rubbish", as you always call it, whenever it impedes your passage through my studio to the window – when you want to open it in the summer, at least, to get some air. Really, it still pains me even to think this much about the apparently "useful items and clippings" that mum used to foist on me whenever I came back to Australia to see her and dad, and now no longer does (obviously). And yet, still, as you would know, all of it – every last bit of what she once gave me – is too unbearable to think about. Always thinking and not thinking about it at the very same time. And so no wonder that you had been trying to suggest a professional service for this house – some kind of "professional rubbish sorter", as you called what is probably better known here as a *de*clutterer or *de*hoarder – this rubbish sorter label you were using that was so much more than I could cope with at the time. How I resented the way you had kept on calling the myriad hoardings of what had accumulated here in this house "rubbish", because what about those photographs and paintings and other precious remnants of the past, as I've described them for you? Those boxes of photographs and letters and journals from my father's parents, for example, who had been living in England during the First World War, before Beryl or dad had even been born? Every one of those boxes that I had found one day, when I was a child, in a cupboard in that room at the end of dad's study – that "junk room", as mum had called it – when I had sat with a torch in the walk-in cupboard so that I could look at as much of it all as I could. Drinking it in. The sense I'd had, even then, of those people whose orderly "Dear Pater and Mater" letter-writing lives were going to be changed in some quiet, brutal and inarticulate way many decades later, as I'd only learned from Beryl one afternoon in her Lindfield flat, not long before she lost her train of thought: the assault (which she was surprised I had never heard a thing about). Do you remember me describing it to you afterwards? At least this *supposed assault* that had left my grandmother just "a shadow of her former self", as Beryl had said, even though she was sure her mother had suffered "no lasting physical damage". The distress of it "passing quickly", too. Yes, this assault that, nevertheless, had left my father "somewhat altered" – which is to say her brother, who was several years younger than her, but suddenly so much "younger-seeming", as Beryl was telling me in the stuffy intimacy of her retirement village flat in Lindfield – this brother that she continued to think of as "*so, so vague*". Yes, thinking again about what had happened to this brother – this father – this *kid*, as I had to think of him now that I was remembering those photographs of his long-legged stepping along with his parents in George Street, Sydney – my father in his dark grey boarding school shorts, his banded straw boater. Those paper receipts for his trumpet that I'd found. For a coat. This still young boy, who had been waiting (as I'd heard from auntie B) in the foyer of his school for a mother who'd returned to the shop where he had left his schoolbag *accidentally*. This father of mine who had been faced, in a way I would have loved to have known a lot more about, with the sudden loss of his bag – his bag and then his mother, perhaps – this mother who was soon to become a "shadow" – and so faced, then, with a lifelong need, indeed an obsession, with keeping everything by him – absolutely everything that he would need for his *interests*, as I remember wondering (albeit in a far more compressed way) for the second or two before my auntie B went on to tell me "other things" about the family and the past. *Her* past, mostly, except for the fights my father used to get into with his ageing and saddening father, most of which I have forgotten now. And yet even before knowing any of these particulars – anything of the story of this supposed assault – my going through all of the letters, receipts, and photographs in the cupboard – pulling them into me – all of this had also been a strangely disturbing experience. These photographs of times that had seemed, even then, so much longer ago than anything I could imagine being connected to in any ordinary sense – these remnants from the people who were connected with this body – *my* body – which was now using its hands, its eyes, to go through these physical traces, where all of it was valuable, as it seemed to me then – and hence even the most torn and useless of the papers valuable. Because how astonished and thrilled I had been to handle even the smallest and least important of my grandparents' bills of travel to Britain during the First World War – and yet despairing too in the very same moment – overwhelmingly despairing – since whatever was I to do with it all? Yes, even then, when I was still that child with the torch in the "junk room" cupboard, I had started to panic about what to do with these physical remnants that had suddenly become only mine to have to deal with. Because how appalling it had been that I should have felt this strongly about pieces of paper that I, myself, might have thrown away if I had just received them – my own bills of travel – in the now of my life, meaning then as a child. Feeling this strongly about *everything* I'd found there in the boxes in the cupboard, and hence everything that dad had taken "holus-bolus" from his parents' house, as mum used to say. These papers and photographs that, as I was working in the hall at dad's place now, and on that first day especially – when the first of the bins was due to arrive – I wouldn't know *what* to do with when I found them again. The horror of finding these boxes of papers, in all likelihood, in the next several days – it being inevitable, surely, that I'd find them soon. The horror of being in such a position, any minute as it seemed, to be handling these ancient papers yet again, and feeling their immense sort of claim on me – the immense, although obscure, demand that would still be attached to all of the papers, let alone what would be attached to the more recent ones, such as those from the sixties, the seventies, the eighties. How all of this paper would have been kept, I knew, in spite of my mother and her intentions – and perhaps even *because of* her intentions. The horror of the collection and her intentions, both. The necessity to harden myself against the enormity of their claims on me. And so this need for me to work, thus, in this "narrow-headed way", as you have called my manner of working at my pieces – my "Still Lives" pieces. This all-or-nothing way of working that I've tended to follow all of my life. And so insistent, as you say, in my methods – insistent in this way that uses the whole of me to focus, to "tunnel through" – not allowing anyone else to get involved, even when they have offered to help. "Pig-headed", you have called it. Pig-headed, perhaps. And yet, I also know very well that it would have been impossible for me to field any of your questions if you had been here with me, helping in the house. Constantly your questions: Do you want this? How about this? And this? All of your too-practical, I-am-just-being-sensible-and-helpful-sounding questions – and the inevitable advice as well. Because just as I knew that I couldn't stand to hear any of your questions about the bags of clothes and clippings that mum used to give me, which were still there in that corner of the studio, I also knew that there was no way – definitely – that I could cope with any such similar questions in the family house. How everything was unbearable. All of it. Which is to say both the thinking about the house and the things in it, and the things themselves – about the *remains*, as I'd been thinking of them, too, since I started working with all of it here. This word "remains": both the remains and the thinking *about* the remains. All of it unbearable. Every bit unbearable.

And so what an astonishing reprieve, as it seemed, at the time, that I'd said what I said to Nathaniel Lord about the *Chatswood Song Dong project*. This idea that had "made it all possible", as I'd said to you afterwards. This idea that, instead of being overwhelmed by what was here in this house – instead of being crushed – so completely overcome – there could now be a way for me to do something *to* it that would transform what I couldn't even bear to think about – yes, all of this stuff – into something different – something that I could live with. Something, in fact, that was *art*. This belief that art could have its *own* solutions to things – its own processes – its very own results, which could not be understood by any other means. Yes, even how, as I remember saying to you on the way to Heathrow on the Tube, that you can be *exposed* to a piece of artwork at only one time in your life and not give that piece of artwork any other attention than this single exposure – nothing more than the fleeting attention of a moment in a gallery – and yet this artwork will, all the same, be starting to squirm its way inside you *without your knowing it* and, in this way and in this way only, soon make it possible for you to *solve, at last, the one huge problem in your life that it has always been impossible to solve.* The serendipity of seeing that Song Dong installation at the Barbican when I did. And then the double serendipity of experiencing how I must have learned something from it – indeed, *taken in* something from it – because, as you see (I said), it had led to that sudden and extraordinary idea emerging from me in the midst of talking to Nathaniel Lord at the gallery in Hackney. Because it was not just a *sort-of* idea – a very vague idea – but an idea that had emerged from me *fully formed.* Telling you all this on the Tube as we were heading out to Heathrow the day that followed the meeting with Lord at the Tate Modern – so excited to be reliving what it had been like for me, for "such an inspired idea" to spring from me *alive* in this way. And yet, in the very same moment that I was telling you about "the perfect timing of it all" – and this *aliveness* – I had actually been remembering, too, how it was, in the gallery in Hackney, that Nathaniel Lord – whom I hadn't seen for decades – decades and decades – had first shown what had looked to be a very strange fixation on my pieces and on me. This way that Nathaniel Lord, which is to say this fearful figure from decades ago in my past, had been so intent on trying to get to the bottom, as it seemed, of what I was doing with my "Still Lives" series – the premise of my approach, as it related both to my previous exhibits and my projected showings – in other words, everything I had been doing and was planning to do with this "Still Lives" series, and of course the Wall. So intent was he that he was practically bending himself over double with the effort of it. You need to be picturing the situation, Teun: Nathaniel Lord, as you might have seen him on that night in Hackney, stooped right over his clear plastic cup of blackish wine, with his over-sized jacket creeping up the back of his wispy white head as I said what I could in response to his peculiarly soft and yet urgent observations and questions about what I'd been doing *with my art*. Yes, this way I'd found myself pressed to say something about how I "continued to be interested in the intrusion of idealised imagery" – this seemingly necessary recourse to the idea of "continuing to be interested" – continuing to be "fascinated" (I even said) with how it is to be "an embodied being in the valencies of the abstractions and substances of the commercialised world". And so instead of avoiding saying any of this in any detail to anyone in person, as I have been managing to do until this moment – only ever writing the correct sort of artspeak in necessary documents, but never saying it face to face to a human being. Instead of doing what I usually do – what I *necessarily do* – since art needs to have its *own* way of being, its *own* way of working, as I've always said – no point in talking about it "if the artwork doesn't speak for itself", as I've often said (to you at least) – instead of this avoidance, I'd been seized, it seemed, by an odd and inexplicable drive to push to the surface every bit of these artspeak notions – these trendy words – that are normally irrelevant and, because irrelevant, so often concocted. To lay before this man, Nathaniel Lord, everything that it might *ever* be possible to say about what I'd been doing with my "Still Lives" series and my projected work on the Wall. And so even the *anorexia*: this word that I have been writing everywhere in my applications and artist's statements – in everything I have been writing in journal pieces these past ten years or more – even pressing to say this word "anorexia" to Nathaniel Lord. This word that I had *particularly avoided* all those years ago in that last-minute project at the end of art school, the last time he might have seen me *in the flesh*, unless it was at one of Sonya's showings – those early showings that I occasionally went to whenever I was back in Australia if it happened to coincide. The awkwardness of being at the very same time compelled to confess, as it were, to the importance, to my "body of work", of my anorexia as well as that student "happening" that he "might remember", and then also, in the short moments afterwards, to attempt to neutralise its relevance to everything since. At the same time overplaying my indebtedness to that "happening" with Eileen and Sonya and – of course – to him (naturally), and conversely, insisting on how it had *only been since arriving in Britain* that I'd been able to turn my work in a "completely different direction", which is to say towards this anorexia slash *post*-anorexia project. And hence towards a much more "subtle exploration" of "these sorts of themes". And so – worst of all – towards the "major expression" I was planning *with that ten-metre Wall*. This capitulation to Nathaniel Lord *yet again*, as it suddenly seemed to me, then, in that instant. This way *yet again* I had let myself tell Nathaniel Lord what I shouldn't have told him – the whole of what was nothing but artspeak. Concocted artspeak. Which is to say how, in the flooding of my panic I had said *far too much* and in such a quantity that it was impossible to retract, impossible to *un*say – the unsaying of it being, precisely, too, the problem. Since the harder I attempted to retract what I'd just said to him about the Wall, and thus its relationship to my "Still Lives" series, the more submerged I was becoming in the mounting incoherence of what I was saying – my attempt to *un*say being far, far worse than the worst of what I had just said to him in the first place. And so how everything I had said and was continuing to say was the very problem I might have avoided if only I could *stop* – this saying that I might never have started to say if Nathaniel Lord hadn't been the one who was trying to get me to say it, as it seemed to me then, at the time – the one who'd kept proffering his brand new gallery space in Eveleigh in what might only have been a joking invitation, if I were to believe his soft little laughs, his so familiar wit and repartee. All of which soon gave rise to those panicky thoughts that kept going around and around in my head as I wondered how it was that, *of all the people* I should have chosen to reveal such spurious, nonsense thoughts to, it was Nathaniel Lord. Since the more he had got me to say about this "Still Lives" Wall – after pressing me to reveal *so much*, as it seemed – *so much* about the project – the worse it became. Since even telling Nathaniel Lord anything at all in the first place – as Sonya has so frequently noticed – is "the kiss of death" for any spark of an idea that a person might have, any idea that this person might want to give form to – and so for anything that he, Lord, as curator and facilitator – writer, academic, and critic – might be tempted to get involved with. Anything at all. Hence it was that every crazy accusation that Sonya has ever posted on Facebook about this one-time mentor of ours from art school had now, somehow, found its noxious way into me as well. Poisoning my thoughts. Every entirely paranoid accusation about what *he had done to her career* – every idea about how, having once been her "champion", as she'd put it – a very brief champion, supposedly, since he had only ever picked up her work just to "fling it away" – that is, having once done the apparently generous and chivalrous thing on her behalf, he had then "set" so many of the galleries in the country "against" her (as she'd written). Every idea that, if you "cross" Nathaniel Lord once, you will never recover from it – that if Nathaniel Lord takes a sudden, unaccountable dislike to you or your work, this dislike will ossify into a *permanent condition*. A permanent judgement. A *personal* judgement now become a supposedly *im*personal judgement. Every idea that even the apparent approbation and support – the enthusiastic support – of Nathaniel Lord and his now very considerable facilities and nous with sourcing the fascinated attention of *an extraordinary variety of private investors* was – all of it – only likely to "doom" you the quicker. The quicker his approbation, the quicker the doom. And so, once a piece or a project had been approved by him, it would never get to thrive since it was only ever half your own work – half of yours and half of his. The spark all yours. The dominance and "absolute falsification" of it (Sonya) his. The way that Nathaniel Lord was only ever interested in directing the "eviscerated puppets" of his *own* vision. "*His Nathaniel Lord vision*". And the minute you dared to think for yourself, you were certain to be tossed and then trodden underfoot. And so it seemed, in that instant, that his persistent interest – his persistent questions, repartee and jokes – had only been designed to catch me out. That he'd only been trying to get me to admit that what I'd been doing in Britain was nothing but an attenuated and even brainless repetition of a project that he liked to believe *he'd* had a hand in developing in the first place – and so trying to get me to admit to the paucity of my work. The *essential paucity*. Getting me to see, too, that even the anorexia angle was but a trivial sort of nothing. An extra nothing. Since the very opacity of the ridiculous expressions I was using – such as this word "valencies" – these expressions that his still highly potent attention had managed to conjure spontaneously, as it were, out of my mouth – "his god-awful presence", as Son would have put it – the very obscure vacancy of all I was saying was simply a sign, as I realised immediately afterwards, that my mind was just as empty as he might have suspected it to be. And so now, desperate to avert the imminent implosion of decades of work, because *still* the food, as I was imagining him thinking. *Still* the bodies. *Still* the obsession with living in a female body among the ongoing onslaught of images of *how we were supposed to be*. Desperate to avert all this, I felt myself pulling into the centre of my being as I attempted to retreat from what I'd just said to him about my "Still Lives" series and the Wall. All of it. The necessity to deny it, suddenly. This Wall about which, until this moment in Hackney with my old art school mentor, I had naturally been cautious about discussing with anyone. Only ever writing about it on my own terms. Only ever in the abstract, and for clear and *practical purposes*. Never discussing it with anyone *in person* – or at least nobody in the art world. Never allowing it, at least, to be discussed by anybody else. This project of the Wall that he was persisting, if only jokingly, in getting me to commit to, there, in London – this Wall that was "perfect" for his new "chic-industrial" space in Eveleigh, as he kept on calling it – alongside the ghosts of the workers, as he said: the ghosts of so many working-class males who would never have seen an anorectic, ever, in their lives. *Imagine it*, he was saying. Tea, bacon, stewed Tasmanian apples. Most of it stodge. *Imagine the smokos*, he was saying. The slabs of butter evaporating in the clouds of nicotine. The waxy cheese. Their "oblivious conversations". And so: *The Song Dong approach* to dad's house. That was how it had arrived in my head. The whole of it there – clear, filled out – in an instant. A desperate plan. And also: the notion of there being no risk *at all* in such a project, as it even seemed to me then. Absolutely none. Since Song Dong, of course, had already taken on the risk himself. *He* had already triumphed – this Song Dong approach to the "problematic material accumulations of twenti-eth-century masculinity" (as I found myself saying eventually, so very easily and naturally) – this same sort of approach and yet with the "masculine and feminine slantings" of his project *reversed* of course, as I said. Yes, you need to imagine how it happened – this way that I was soon telling Nathaniel Lord that, "prior" to the construction of the Wall, I was intending to make "a very different sort of artwork". How I was *even then* in the midst of *early preparations* for "taking a Song Dong approach" to the leavings of my "recently deceased father in Sydney" whose peculiar obsessions "had always been expressed in a minutely purposeful drive for perfection and detail" – in the labelling, for instance, of all of his books and magazines with the Dewey decimal system (as it came to me then). *A mania for labelling.* The labelling of every disposable pen he had ever refilled with ink, every electric light bulb he had replaced, with the date and brand name of the item he had used. The progressive accumulation, I had said – and over many, many decades – of an "extraordinary and complex system" that was only in fact dwarfed by a system – similarly immense – of "complete disorder". The one and the other – the one pitted against the other, as I said. An incredible tension between them. The one trying to *overtake* the other, to swallow the other with its "disturbingly encyclopaedic dimensions", its complete and utter filth and chaos. The extreme proliferation of *objects*, I said – this word "objects" being one of Nathaniel Lord's favourite words, as I'd even remembered from the art history tutorials I had taken with him at art school. Yes, you should have seen the way that the eyes of my one-time teacher had narrowed and grown moist as he took in what I was offering him *over and above* my descriptions of the Wall: this image of a vast accumulation of objects and filth, and in such an array – the very scale of the profusion and disorder and also, perhaps, unlikely treasures, in the house and life and being of my father. All of it striking Nathaniel Lord in a positive way, as it seemed at the time – the very same monumentally terrifying image of the house and its contents, which, until the moment when I began to describe it to him, which is to say only a matter of days before I was to fly back to Sydney, was something I hadn't been able to bear thinking about in any way at all.

And so the relief. Such an immense relief, I remember telling you over and over again on the Tube to Heathrow. Such an extraordinary relief that I had come up with this "incredible solution" – where I seemed to be speaking of it to you – of this supposed solution – as if I had *already* finished the project and so *already dealt with the problem of the house*. As if I had *already* made that "massive and interesting artwork" at Thinkspate Galleries that was going to be "on the scale of Song Dong's most famous piece that had travelled the world" – this artwork which, as Nathaniel Lord had said in the meeting that followed it in the Tate Modern Café, he would be "so proud" to be in a position to host "on an appropriate scale". How he was almost chuckling with the audacity of what I was doing. My "*unfilial audacity*", as he'd put it with his cheeks crinkling up and back into his crumpled, skin-flecked corduroy collar. And yet the scale of my blindness then, Teun. My conscious blindness. Since, in this short time before I left for Australia, I was no longer thinking of dad as I had known him – no longer trying to remember what I could of how he had always been for me – the complexity of everything I could recall about him, which was now becoming less and less complex the more I tried to haul it up. No longer even trying to have a view – any view at all – of the sum of these worn-out thoughts about him, because I was now taken up with the prospect of "soon knowing my father better than I had ever known him". As if, with this project, there were going to be no barriers or problems – only bene-fits – only the salutary benefits – of "taking full stock of my father's mind". Yes, I remember that I even wondered out loud to you on the Tube why it was that I had not understood any earlier how such *an ethical and orderly approach* would be so necessary to "this sort of difficulty", as I was calling it. And my wondering, too, how it had taken me *this long* to develop some "appropriate" way of approaching it all – this problem of my parents and their "stuff" that has dogged me the whole of my life. In fact, why was it, I remember asking you, that my father had to die just as my mother had to die before I could begin to make any sense of what I'd seen in The Curve at the Barbican – in other words, before I could see there was meaning and value "in every bit of the stuff" that they'd left behind them? Every bit of that *shit*, I think I even said by way of explanation, that our parents inev-itably leave, but which, of course, they would have preferred to be able to see – and to be alive in order to see – that *we*, their children, could finally understand. And this way that I'd used the word shit to mean *so much more* than rubbish, as I could only see over here while I was working in the hall of the family home in Chatswood – this distance I had, now, on the wheeling of my thoughts as they'd been turning and turning as we sat on the Tube, heading out to Heathrow. Not the word "rubbish" that *you* had used, Teun, of course. Our parents go through their lives building a nest of shit around them, I remember saying as we were travelling on the Tube out to Heath-row together (through a tunnel that was lined with the grey and crusted arteries of all sorts of piping) – something about growing up in that shit. *Being made of shit.* Okay, I probably didn't say shit then. I think I wanted to, but I couldn't, probably. I might have said crap or just *stuff.* All these Aussie-style words that I would have been hesitant to use at all if Nathaniel Lord hadn't made it so easy for me to think again in this way, when he had approved of what I was planning to do – through my "very Australian suburban perspective" – this seemingly random and irrelevant idea about "applying a *Song Dong solution*" to the house. Telling you about how, in such a view – in such a Song Dong–inspired view – everything had value. Even the worst of the crap in a place like this had value. Just as, "for the whole of my life" (as I said to you), I had *known* that it did. How I "longed" to get here, to Sydney, to begin on this project. Even the most abject of this stuff can be beautiful or at least *presented as beautiful,* I remember telling you when we'd got to Heathrow and were standing at one of those raised little table-and-stool sets near an advertisement for luggage after I'd checked in my bags – one of those crazy advertisements, as I'd said, since obviously it was far too late to do anything about buying new luggage just then. Song Dong's mother, I was reminding you – since you hadn't seen the exhibition at the Barbican but had only heard about it through me and Arijit – mostly through Arijit, I'm fairly sure – this mother of Song Dong's had collected so many crappy plastic bottles and so many crappy plastic lids, so many empty tubes. Practically empty. Nothing but crap, the lot of it, but clearly nothing that couldn't also become entirely beautiful when it had been arranged in such a way that the whole collection could be viewed as a massive work of art, in both its detail and design – "a sensitive reworking of her life and experience", as I or probably Arijit, earlier, had described it to you, you'd said. And of course, nothing in this exhibition was disgusting to me. It was surprising, I said, because not a single bit of the exhibition had been disgusting in any way at all. Even the most abject and useless and worn of the objects was beautiful, I remember saying – each of those worn and probably still smelly pairs of shoes, those balls of wool, those flattened-out tubes. The soap with the long, deep cracks that were filled to the surface with grime – one after the other. One alongside the other. And so it was that this beauty of the whole thing, the entire installation, had made me revise (I'd said) what I had been tending to say to everyone – our friends – about the *stuff* in my parents' house – which had made me think about my parents' house and its contents "in an entirely *other way*". How excited I had been that Nathaniel Lord was so keen to "facilitate this project", which was going to be important in developing understanding, in Australia, of these sorts of *ordinary suburban leavings*. Yes, everything seemed to have lined up for me with this project. It was going to bring *everything* in my life together.

I had a sense then, as I was about to walk onto the plane at Heathrow, that soon "so much" would be revealed and I would come to know what *it all meant* – this sense that the burden of the house, which was filled with "rubbish", as you called it, was about to be transformed through a sensitive and orderly artistic practice – a *culturally attuned* artistic practice – into a "collection" that would simply be made up of a variety of ordinary objects that had, in fact, "always been brilliant". Always been diverse and interesting. All of it soused and heavy and shiny with the kind of meaning that was about to reveal itself for what, essentially, it *was*. That – basically – this Song Dong–inspired approach was little more than a "practice" that would enable me to see how the ordinary filth of life – that is, the stuff in the family home, with its layers of bodied and *dis*embodied human existence – all of it *in* the filth, or rather *in* the objects – a part of the objects – how this deceptively simple approach could become a methodical means of "celebrating this brilliance" (I said). And so everything I'd feared earlier – everything I had avoided – could be included as well. That is, all of my guilt and difficulty could be flipped inside out and *made to do its thing*. Because it was not at all that I was "in denial" about what I would soon be discovering to be the essential ordinariness of the objects I was about to be finding and sorting, I said, when we'd moved to that sort-of café in Heathrow – when you were looking at your phone and getting anxious that I should already be moving towards the gates – getting anxious but not saying anything just yet, as you never like to do. Not at all that I was "in denial".

I was sitting there, still, with my coffee not yet finished – and with my toast not yet finished (as surely you will remember) – and I was saying how I was already beginning to imagine how easy it might be to arrange *all of the news-papers* somehow – and to lay out, over the floor, *all of the stained and unwanted clothing*. All of dad's notes. His piles of magazines and books. All of those volumes that had been labelled so beautifully on the spines with his meticulous rendering of letters and numbers. His shaky hand. All of his socks. To arrange every last bit of the contents of the house so that it would be "beautiful, brilliant, and moving". And that the very act of its all being appreciated and acknowledged in this way, or in fact even *before* it was arranged – the intention to arrange it and so to acknowledge it, would already be "half the work", since this was what I had realised "only recently" when I'd brought, to my interest in Song Dong's "emotional achievement", as it related to his mother and his family story, something of the "object-oriented sympathies" of the tidiness guru Marie Kondo (do you remember how I'd been reading her book that time, when I was "trying to make an effort" with the studio?). Yes, bringing in something of that: her tenderness with the objects, each of the objects, no matter that, surely, when all of them had been massed together, they would threaten to block out the sky. And so, drawing on the two of them, then, for my *suburban Chatswood project* – the tender-hearted discarder as well as the collector. And I had a sense, now, of how it would be possible to arrange the contents of the house in *small aesthetic collections*, which would then guarantee the success – the perfect success – of the project – the *act* of approaching it all in this multi-pronged sensitive way being essential to the success of the whole (do you remember how I had gone on and on about how each bit of the various leavings – even the *worst of the leavings*, the ugliest of the leavings – needed to be "acknowledged"?). And how I'd also realised that there was "so much in the house" that was *already* beautiful and interesting – so many of the books that were *bona fide* interesting in the most ordinary and obvious sense. So many of the plates and ornaments and wooden chairs with the dust growing black and thick in the creased inlets of their carvings – all of these bits and pieces beautiful and interesting "in themselves". I was so fired up then – I know – as I sat with you in that café-sort-of-place at Heathrow that it was hard to talk about anything else. Too hard to contain how excited I was feeling. And even though I could tell that you were already growing sick of responding to what I was saying but were loath to tell me – don't make me say it, I imagined you saying, if you'd had to – if, in fact, I'd pressed you. And yet I'd kept on talking about it all nonetheless. I had kept on talking about this Song Dong idea. *This Song Dong Chatswood project*. Yes, I remember saying that I was still trying to understand how it was that it had taken me *this long* to even begin to see how such an approach as Song Dong brings to "these kinds of problems" might be important – even *relevant* to me. How this sudden realisation about the house and the Song Dong approach had given me a "means" of making sense of everything about my life that I had found, thus far, so very difficult to face. And yet, I could also see that it was a simple concept – a perfectly clear and flexible but nonetheless "straightforward" concept that I might even have come up with myself *if I'd put my mind to it* (this I had said). And it was then that I started to say how *odd* it was that I hadn't understood, when I had first seen Song Dong's work, how very relevant to me his aesthetic approach would be – his practical face-to-face way of working with a whole manner of ugly and broken objects. Because, as you knew, I had *long* been worried about what I was going to do with the house and its contents when my parents died. In fact (I said), I remember telling you how I had not looked too closely at the exhibition when it had come to the Barbican all those years ago. Our friend Arijit had asked me to go with him to see it, so I did as he said, do you remember? Going principally to accompany Arijit, our old friend, who always hates going to shows on his own – going, too, as a useful way of socialising with him because he is so busy these days and keeps putting us off. All of us busy. Our sense of never being able to do all the things we want to do. All the months and years passing. So many shows that we miss. And I remember how he, Arijit, had spent so much longer in The Curve, looking at all of the objects and patterns, than I did – Arijit lingering for a very long time by certain of the pieces that Song Dong and his family had assembled for us there in the Barbican – Arijit spending so much longer and looking in far more detail than I had been able to bother with doing myself. In fact, I remember only being *sort of interested* when I was looking at it all – how I had even feigned my interest in the show on the day that Arijit and I met up at the Barbican before going on to lunch to gossip about friends before he went back to his work. Yes, at the airport, I was remembering how I'd told you, not long after this visit to the gallery, that Arijit had always been so much more interested in the sorts of things that *I* should have been interested in myself – Arijit, not being an artist, of course, which made it all the worse. I knew you really didn't have much time for Arijit when he talked about artworks and films in the way that he did. Arijit was *my* old friend, not yours, and so it made sense that *I* was the one who went along with him to shows. Okay (I'd said), Arijit really didn't know what he was talking about when he said the kinds of things that were calculated to show you and me up as a pair of stuck-in-the-mud thinkers – the kinds of thinkers who only *thought* we were creative – always *saying* we were creative, but were never actually interested in what was "really" happening in the *creative world*. Arijit, since he is a dermatologist and not an artist, as you have always pointed out, didn't have to think about risking himself and his innermost obsessions and interests – never having to put out into the world a single twisted image of the workings of his mind – never having to offer a single original thought. So it made sense that he had *loads of time* to be looking around him in this *judgemental way*. He could take his pick. He didn't have to think about his next assignment, his latest creative commitment, as you did in your job. No designs for engineering companies, for instance, that could only be finished by suppressing every single creative thought that had just been stirred – by stamping on, suffocating, every wavering thought, as you did every day of your life. The everyday compromise, you have often said, of the working, jobbing artist (I reminded you). Arijit had so much more freedom to do what he wanted to do and to think how he wanted to think, you had said as we sat there with our coffees at the airport (yours finished long ago). The whole world was spread out for his delectation and he could look at or think about it all as a connoisseur does – yes, a connoisseur who can close his eyes and take his time. So it was no wonder, as you said to me then, that my reactions to artworks were not going to be the same as Arijit's – saying all this as if the irritation you were clearly feeling about Arijit and his pretentions to know what was what in the world of art was really just the irritation you were reluctant to admit to about me and the ideas I'd been battering you with the whole way into Heathrow, as I was preparing to leave for Australia and the house.

And in the house itself: as I kept pulling more and more of the stuff out from the hallway – still trying to avoid the pathetic sight of that bit of carpet and the writing desk – determined to ignore the horror of the carpet and the desk – I found myself reflecting on how any of this had come about – this taking over of my mind by the Song Dong idea. And so working to understand how the Song Dong show at the Barbican had even come into my mind at the opening in Hackney in the first place. Of how it had declared itself when I was speaking to Nathaniel Lord about my plans and projects, and declared in such a way that it had clearly come across – both to him and me – as a considered and thoughtful idea, and hence not at all as one that had just fallen into my head from somewhere else. This idea or, rather, lie about how this particular Song Dong notion had been obsessing me for years – this out-and-out lie about how I had "long been affected" by the work of "this fascinating conceptual artist" Song Dong and, therefore, "long" been trying to work out how "the essence of his approach" might be applied to "a very different context". This appalling lie that had not seemed, at the time, to be such a lie at all – just a coming-to-an-understanding. A growing understanding. Since it had seemed, then, that this thought about the objects and the stuff in the house had sprung from my brain as if it had *always* lived there – grown from its centre, as if from a seed. Nurtured in that sheltering dark for a very long time.

And yet, if I try to think about what else might have led me to say all this to Nathaniel Lord (I was thinking here in the family home the day that the first of the skips was due to arrive), all I can think of is how it was not so long before the opening in Hackney that I was seized, as it seemed, by the conviction that something was wrong with my "Still Lives" pieces. The individual pieces. Too late, you were saying when you saw how I had got out the methylated spirits and was trying to remove what I'd described as the "appalling grime" that had accumulated between the layers – this way I had decided, perhaps unwisely, to pull apart all of the sheets of perspex and glass and steel and the netting of wires that I had assembled in the months beforehand – pulling them apart so that I could clean in the creases as well as between the layers. Removing every bit of what turned out to be the imaginary dust and oil that had supposedly jammed into the inside grooves and fissures, into the threads of the screws. Filming the glass. How much duller the layers had been looking, I remember thinking before I did it. So obscure the effect. And yet that was how it had been, I was thinking again now as I moved these larger pieces – all of these clearly extraneous pieces – from the space that was opening up in the hall. And yet (I thought as I moved) I also remember thinking about the funeral I'd missed, and of Beryl's daughter and of Angus while I was working on the supposed last-minute clean-up of my "Still Lives" pieces. Yes, most of the time thinking about anything other than the works themselves as I was wiping away at the grime that might have been there, and then playing with the angles of the sheeting as I worked to put the pieces back together in what was probably a breathless, haphazard manner – this way I'd decided to adjust what I had already finished many months earlier and which I shouldn't have been fiddling with *this* close to the show. And so this familiar mode of getting caught up with what I am doing, or at least what it is that I *think* I am doing. That is, continuing a long and obsessive thought to its logical conclusion. And this is what I was thinking again, Teun, as I pulled more and more of the stuff from the hallway out of dad's place. More of the "rubbish", as you would have called it: an old-style metal cupped radiator, probably from the fifties or sixties, with its black and white–banded electrical cord fraying as I pulled on it – fraying to reveal its inner stained twist of coloured wires as I pulled it out from under a nest of what might have been the contents of a wardrobe: a tangle of coat hangers (plastic, metal, wooden). Belts and blue-mouldered, whitish bags. Then a large and leaning stack of chipboard shelving that crumbled as it moved. Grabbing as much as I could of the pieces, the broken pieces – the tangled and scattering pieces – and pulling them out and down across the teeth of the steps to the remnant of lawn out the front.

When I stood near the driveway again, staring for a bit at the road and the cars, I realised I could hear, over the thudding rhythm of my heart, the falling, chirping sound of a bird that must have bothered me when I used to live there. As well as knowing it was a familiar call – such a familiar descent of separated notes – I also knew that I had never in my whole life caught any sight of this irritating bird that was always sending its persistent chirps from the highest tops of the trees around the house, at least as it seemed to me then – chirping with its tediously long and drawn out intervals back when I was a child just as it was doing so again – as if this bird had never once stopped in its daily, ordinary and wearisome work in all of the years I wasn't around to hear it. And so it was while I was looking up into the thick grey branches of the camphor laurels – these American-looking trees that might not have been American at all, I was thinking – looking as carefully as I could so that I might catch sight of the bird whose call, I realised, didn't match with any names of species I might have recognised – none of the *more obvious Australian birds*. None of those calls that I knew and would have recognised in an instant, even if I was never able to imitate them (naming them as I have always done for our friends in London – and for you as well). Not a magpie, I had been thinking, not a currawong – not even what I remembered to be a noisy miner or a koel or a butcherbird. Yes, it was while I was looking up, straining my neck, so that I might see what had prodded into my head on so many mornings of my life, as it suddenly seemed – hearing but never knowing what this annoying bird was – that a roar started up from the house to the right as I stood there – a screeching roar – and I could see that, behind the scrags of brown-headed hydrangea bushes with their bright green spears clustering in their midst, the neighbour

– one of them – perhaps the husband of that couple I remembered – perhaps Mr Mason – who would have been ancient now – someone with wide blue jeans – had opened the driver's side of a car in their driveway to vacuum inside it, huddled over the machine so that it looked as if it were only the legs doing the vacuuming. Making this noise. This noise that obliterated the dredge of that chirping bird, and that reminded me then of dad as he used to wedge himself under the car to work on it, his navy blue overalled legs sticking out and slightly bent, like the legs of a doll. And so, as I went back inside, into the house, I found myself wondering all over again why it was that I'd even thought to bring Song Dong and his work – and thus his *approach* – to this house and this life that I still didn't understand so well. Song Dong, whose work had developed in a very different place, and in a world with much more obvious and serious problems. Okay, Nathaniel Lord had seemed to be "onto" me – pressuring me, as it had felt, but why think of Song Dong and his work at such a time? In fact, when I tried then to remember how it was just before the opening in Hackney – before this show that I should never have bothered to turn up to if I'd had my priorities "properly sorted", as you'd even said to me on the night – nothing specific came to my mind. Probably, I was thinking, I was still immersed in my incomprehension that dad had just died. Also, there was the sting from what Beryl's daughter Kate had said about missing the funeral – fears about Angus, too. Probably guilt. Treating you to the results of my "paranoid over-think-ing", as you've kept on calling what I was saying back then when I tried to surmise what "had really happened" in the weeks and months leading up to my father's death. Telling you about it all, no matter how impatient you seemed when I kept going over and over what everyone had said – what everyone had done or not done. Those thoughts that I "persisted" in shar-ing (as you put it, I remembered). *All of them baseless suppositions*, as you tried to get me to see. And how irritated you were when I kept "harangu-ing our friends" with my theories about Angus and that daughter of Beryl's (Kate, unless it had been Clair). And yet, all the same, you still went on to tell all the people we knew about how "hurt" I had been at *the way I'd been treated by all the idiots in my family.* And then came "the Hackney show", or so we'd been calling the thing since first I heard of it – this show whose opening event I should never have gone to. All so unfortunate, you were saying. Because if I had really wanted to fly back to Australia, I should have "definitely" done so straightaway, the minute I heard that dad had died. Everyone would have understood *completely* if I hadn't turned up, you had said. *No one* would have expected me to go to the opening "at a time like this". But if I didn't intend to leave for Australia then, I should at least have been active in making sure my pieces were hung in the way they that should have been hung. This was where you *really couldn't understand me at all,* as you were saying on the day of the opening, I then remembered, when we'd arrived to find that the pieces had been moved – and moved to the back of the gallery – into that darkish corner with the over-strong spots, which was probably just practical of the owners, as I had then said (when I'd been compelled to defend them – the owners – to you), since it would have been difficult and cumbersome to get around the pieces, due to the way they needed to be suspended *away* from the wall. Much more "practical", I had said, even though it was also true I had been upset. Because now, in this new position, the pieces were close – yes, *far too close* – to the table with the drinks and that doorway that led to the toilets. *Right at the back.* How hurt I had been, you could see (you said). How wronged, how "used". But if I had "actually cared" about my pieces and where they needed to be hung, *I would have already been onto the gallery owners.* I would in fact have stayed all day at the gallery rather than going home when I did. I would have "definitely" made sure that the gallery owners weren't going to be able to override so easily what it was that I had already stipulated earlier and, indeed, what I had already done with the pieces. I would have "definitely" told them" about what had happened with my dad and his death and all "the stress surrounding his death", as you described it in such a simple and straightforward way (as I should have been able to do for myself). Clearly I didn't care enough, you even told me in the car while you were driving us home on the evening of the opening – when I was still unable to say why it was that I was in "such a mood". Because if I didn't care enough about my pieces to care about how they were hung – if I didn't put in the most minimal effort to do this – how *on earth* could I expect anybody else to do it for me? How on earth could anybody at all in the world ever think of me and my needs or preferences, as you had said at last when you turned the engine off – becoming angry suddenly and hitting the steering wheel with the heel of your hand. How on earth could anyone ever do the exact right thing by me if I didn't even bother to do it for myself?

As more of the walls in dad's place were becoming visible – visible, although damp and sloughing and hence very different from what I had been expecting to find – it came to me that the thingness of the house was as much of a problem as the stuff inside it. It was as if, with the ground pushing up through the cracks in the render – the green-black tidal foam – as if what I was dealing with here was not so much a house and its contents as a slow retreat of one thing into another – bricks into soil into moss into pit into hole. And so it began to be clear – as the house itself seemed already to be challenging what I remembered of its greyish Hoover-smelling corridors, the lead-tasting paint on the sill in my bedroom, the soundless sighing of the trees on the other side of the glass in their aluminium edges – that I really had no idea what it was I was trying to get at with this *Song Dong solution*, since the house as an object wasn't there at all in that Song Dong exhibition in the Barbican, or at least as I remembered it. The structure, yes. The skeleton, yes. But nothing of its thingness. Nothing of its moods. And so it was that I could only see now, in this house, that I would never have been able to leave out the thingness of the house itself – that the house was just as important, if not far more important, than the things inside it. But also that I couldn't have known that I would feel this way until I'd seen and felt it for myself. That the problem of the house as an object – as a mood, as a smell – would, if I hadn't *already* decided to leave it be and call it quits, have brought me up short and exposed my quote-unquote long-thought-out plans for the place – my artistic plans – as the lies that they were. Because, yes, I had been in *deep* with the lies. In fact, I remember being *so* intent on saying to you, on the evening of the meeting with Nathaniel Lord and then, the very next day, on the Tube, that – despite and somehow in complete contradiction to what I'd also been saying about my desultory experience with Arijit at the show – despite all this, I'd been "struck" when I saw the Song Dong exhibition in the Barbican – struck, because it was only *then* that I "realised" that I'd been thinking about something "close to this sort of thing" for several years now. And I even said that this was a thought that was only "confirmed" that time I visited dad and Angus after mum had died – the visit that followed a matter of months after seeing Song Dong's show. The death and the show, which I was seeing as "tied together in an emotional sense". But of course, my mother was not yet dead when I saw the show. There'd been no sense of a death at the time. In fact, all I had thought about when I saw it (apart from my irritation with Arijit – my clear irritation with his relative openness and receptiveness) was how envious I had been of Song Dong and his mother – so envious of the way *he* had been able to work closely with his mother. Thinking of this relationship, then, and what they had been able to do together – more about this relationship than the results of their work as such. The extraordinary achievement that Song Dong had managed to effect in his relationship with his mother. His magnanimous relationship. His persistence and care. His capacious and resilient vision. Yes, all I had – I was thinking in the house in Chatswood – was a definite idea of what I, myself, was *unable* to do – a sense that I *should* have been capable of initiating such a project with my *own* mother. Isn't anyone capable? But clearly I was not capable of doing this in any kind of way. Because, unlike Song Dong and his mother, my mother and I had never "seen eye to eye". Even the *first* step in the process of consultation would have been impossible – the very thought of its being possible was definitely impossible. And so although I had said to you in Heathrow that it would have been *ideal* to have begun this project several years earlier, when both of my parents were still alive, I also knew that I would never have been able to manage such a thing in practice, since the feelings I had about this house and its problems, and myself as connected to this house and its problems, were far too intense – far too frightening – ever to get close to. This realisation, then, in my parents' house, that I would have had to rely, in order to carry out my supposed *Song Dong Chatswood project*, on the complete oblivion of my parents *to* this project – on their *necessary oblivion*. Because even when mum had died, there was still my father alive – this father who, when mum had gone, spread the remnants of everything he did and everything he thought about – all of it – over the house. In every room, on every surface. So that soon there was nothing left of my mother that you could easily see anymore. My father obliterating all apparent traces of my mother in the house, with all of his projects that were always "in train". The house – this five-bedroom house – being far too small, as he would constantly say, to contain the breadth and details of his "important ideas" that were still evolving, at least in his mind. And so in The Curve, as you can imagine, I might have been thinking of my parents, or at least of my mother, when I had seen what Song Dong had constructed out of the remnants of his mother's existence – this woman's "carefully prudent existence", as Arijit had described it so appreciatively to me at the time – "careful" and "prudent" being positive words in his vocabulary. Everything about Arijit and his family being positive in this way, if you think of it, Teun. And so my envy – of Song Dong and his mother and, of course, of Arijit and his mother, too: that time I had seen her at Arijit and Franz's place – the way she had sorted through Arijit's (admittedly) extraordinary collection of Edwardian cutlery to find us a matching set for dinner. Her large-armed capacity for doing just this, for picking over his spoons with such generous decisiveness. How she could easily sort between those that "worked" with the cloth on the table and those that "didn't". Arijit and his mother, what's more, who were always engaged in improving on that astonishing collection of ferns and orchids that you would have seen in Arijit and Franz's conservatory – a collection that had started (as I heard) from his mother's collection. My envy of Arijit and his mother, as I have been thinking of it recently, joining up with my envy of Song Dong and his mother. My envy of their way of living. The thought that I might have been able to live in this world if only I had made *the necessary effort* – if only I had been able to resist every urge of mine to block or avoid – the Song Dong experience being mostly an envious experience for me at the time. This sense, too, that if only I had been able to push myself *to* it, I would surely have thought of this *interesting take* on a lifetime of hoarding – so definitely thought of it, first, myself. And yet it's true, that despite all this terrible envy, I had made sure I conceded to Song Dong and his pre-eminent vision. Indeed, I had said to you, very simply I think, that the Song Dong *Waste Not* show in 2012 had "struck a chord in me". The permission that it gives, as I think I said to you as well at Heathrow – how "so much becomes possible" – yes, trying to convey to you, as we were hanging around in that coffee-serving place, waiting for the time I needed to leave – to do all this – about how amazed I'd been. Amazed and confused. That when I had seen this show – this *Waste Not* show – it had actually suggested to me (I said) *everything* that I had been trying to get at in these frustrating years since leaving Australia – in fact, since I began all this work on my "Still Lives" pieces – these "preparatory pieces", as I tended to call them – at least to you. Always a preparation for something else. Because only now could I see that these "preparatory pieces" had been "laying the ground" for me to do this important artwork *all along* – this final and brilliant installation (I was saying). This *all-encompassing work of art* that would combine everything that was important to me.

Ha! When I think now about how it took you some time to come around to seeing what I was trying to tell you, it's hard not to smile. You'd resisted for a while, I was remembering as I kept on at the work with the clutter in the hallway in Chatswood – in fact, while I was pulling out a stack of polystyrene boxes that were mostly filled with papers and plastic bags and sleeves and all sorts of twisted bits of things that were easy to remove. Yes, the harder you pushed, the stronger was the need in me to push right back at you – with you pushing against, and me counter-pushing with even the least of what I was claiming for my work and my life from the Song Dong approach (its benefits for my work as a whole, as I'd been trying to argue

– the direction of my work – plus the "soundness" of what I was calling its "ontological position" – the "ever-shifting *modalities*" too, as I think I'd called it, of a family in the time and place it had "flourished" in, as I said – and so in *suburban* Sydney from the sixties until now). Really, the harder you pushed, the harder, the stronger, the more determined *I* was in pushing back, in trying to justify what I'd done in committing to this *Song Dong–inspired exhibition* with Nathaniel Lord. Yes, and – conversely – the more I tried to explain why it was important to me – *vitally important* – the more you questioned everything I was saying. And yet, all this meant that I soon became more and more determined *not* to let you speak. Because I *had* to convince you. I had to insist that I'd actually been thinking about something like this for a *very* long time. That the problem of the house and my inheritance from the house – from my parents – from everyone in the family, in the house, who had since "passed on" – had long been troubling me. That I'd *always* been trying to solve it, trying to use the whole of my artist's intelligence to solve what had always seemed impossible to solve "until now". In fact, telling you that *this* was why I had run away from home, from Australia, at the end of the eighties. Telling you this after you'd come back from the office some hours after I'd returned home from the meeting with Nathaniel Lord at the Tate Modern, even getting hot in the face as I was saying it – this memory of getting hot in the face and determined to convince you being associated with our kitchen, where you soon started making your usual combination – your usual *pilav*, as you call it. All the little bowls of chopped vegetables. Grated carrot with black seed and lemon juice. Squares of green peppers. That gently oily mixture of rice that I've never been able to make without its burning at the bottom of the pan, and so always avoiding attempting to make myself. In case I get it wrong. Trying to get you to see, to agree with me, that my "whole life" as an adult had indeed been spent in trying to solve this problem of "the house" – my urge to keep running away from it – from everyone *in* it – that was never going to be solved through what I was doing with my "bitsy" approach to the panels, let alone "my surviving anorexia Wall", this "Still Lives" Wall

I was yet to make. But even if a very small part of what I'd been trying to get you to believe was true – even if the problem of the house had indeed been occupying me for the largest part of my life, and even if the Song Dong approach had "resonated" with me, as I think I said, I can now say for certain that the work of Song Dong – everything about it – his famed acknowledgement and treatment of his mother's anxiety and her house and its cultural and historical context – his sensitive tribute to this chapter of Chinese social history – was actually very far from the front of my mind that evening, at the opening of the show in Hackney. It certainly wasn't a project I was thinking about as I walked through the gallery, from the doors at the front – on the street – to the back where it seemed that my pieces had been moved to. Those fraught minutes while I scanned the walls, the corners, looking for the pieces – ignoring the people. Getting there last, once Suz had got me to look. Making my way eventually to the spot where the pieces were hanging in the very back section of the gallery, where I resigned myself to lingering not too far away from the pieces, and so waiting, as usual, for someone to approach me with the kinds of gossipy conversations about life – art – the art world – that we tend to make on evenings like these. Waiting close but not too close to the pieces. You know how it is. You'd gone out to the front of the gallery again to start from the beginning, as I remember – "to see everything", as you so generously said, but I knew I was not in a mood even to pretend to be interested in anyone else, let alone in their works, so I hung around near my pieces in the back room, but not too near. Trying to make myself think that the panels looked a lot less neglected and less depressing than I feared – less neglected, that is, than I thought they looked when I first walked in to see that they were hanging exactly where Suz, one of the gallery owners, had said she thought "would be best for the pieces". This place "all on their own", as she said when she saw me arrive, which had sounded, right from the first, so very dismissive. The language of specialness, of care and thoughtfulness, but actually a dismissal. A *blatant dismissal.* The "best position", as Suz had just said, which of course meant that it was definitely the worst position in the entire gallery. This Suz talking to me as if I were an idiot – a complete idiot – as if she could see how her persuasive language was working in the way she knew it would – watching how I had nodded and seemed to be happy as I kept on moving past her. Seemed to be convinced. Yes, this Suz, this gallery owner secure in thinking that she – they – had *done* the "right thing" by me and my works. So very thoughtfully thinking about the *needs of the pieces*. Suz definitely appearing to me then as both smug and convinced by the generous care that she, and so they (she and Clem, her partner), "extended to all their artists". Hence the despair I was feeling. The despair at my works. Trying to make myself believe, then, that my pieces weren't quite as awful as they appeared to be in that instant. And, beneath this, my fury with the owners of the gallery – that is, my fury with Suz – her large, white-spectacled persistence, her way of peering through those massive frames as she spoke, her startled-looking doggedness. My fury with Clem as well – the supposedly practical and thoughtful Clem – always so busy and thanking people "ever so much". Always making sure that I, we, could *see* that she was busy. Her way of moving around the space with such care, such earnest grace – such an attentive and over-articulated concern, as if the whole purpose of this exhibition in Hackney – in this baby that was their gallery – both Suz's and Clem's – as if everything she, Clem, did was just to make sure that we could see and acknowledge that *she was exerting her all* – that she was definitely busy. That no matter what I thought of what she was doing – or what any of us thought – none of us could ever reproach her for not *busting her gut*, as we'd call it in Oz. Driven to the bone with every single thing that she did. Hence my fury with this pair of anxious, devious owners, as it was striking me there in the gallery as I stood not too far away from my pieces, those sad-looking things that I suddenly loathed. And so to cover over all this fury and embarrassment – the embarrassment that was the fury – I made myself move off to get a drink from the table, from where Clem, as I could see, was of course busy lining up the cups of differently coloured wine and soda water and orange juice in a beautiful arrangement – as if only to demonstrate that she was *on top of this task*. Absolutely on top of it. And so there could be *no way* that I could be annoyed with how things were working out that evening in the Hackney Space of Nine. Since, clearly, there was not a thing – no possible thing – that could be further squeezed from her capacity to do her *very best*. Trying *my* best not to show that I couldn't bear to be put in this position, as it felt, of having to appear to approve of her overwhelming tense-necked breaking-guts busyness. Having to appraise it and approve it, and also – adding to the impossibility of my position, as I saw it – having then to compose my face, in case Clem looked up from her cups and bottles to see me standing there – so she'd be reassured – composing my face so as to communicate to her, and thus to both her and Suz, that I was the kind of artist who was "cool to work with", who was *of course* very grateful and happy about everything she and Suz had done for me. Since they had obviously been *killing* themselves *to be fair to us all.* You need to understand how it was for me in those long ten minutes or so before I finally twigged that the morose-looking figure that was hanging around at the time in the periphery of my vision – one of those heavy, dull-looking figures, of the kind I instinctively avoid – was actually someone I knew. Yes, one of those fussily down-dressed society peers, as it might have seemed that he was, in his over-washed brown corduroy jacket in the gallery, if I had bothered to look at him squarely when I'd first noticed him there. Of the sort that looked like he was itching to accost anyone who was standing near him – haranguing anyone that might have been up to listening to any long bit of wisdom he wanted to share. Always referring to "Mother with her Constables and Sargents" – those Constables and Sargents that in fact, as he would claim, embarrassed him *immensely*. One of those figures on his jaunt to the oh-so-edgy east, or even one of the many self-consciously *arty* baby-boomers with their *loads of money* and only a belated interest in art now that they have retired and grown sick of Spain. Or even one of those self-consciously rejuvenated and yet still highly depressive *out there* subscribers to any of the Hackney Space of Nine "events". And so how it was before I finally twigged that this figure was none of these usual sorts but instead someone I knew and – more than this – the very someone that it might have mattered to me to see in this place at all, if I'd ever been asked to choose such a person – absolutely anyone – which is to say, my supposed art school rescuer and inspiration: my teacher-cum-mentor, Nathaniel Lord. For years and years you fantasise about running into someone like this from your past – someone who would be "so surprised" to see where you'd got to. Someone who, as you hope – as you expect – would express their instant admiration of what you are doing – their being so completely overcome (as you hope) that they wouldn't know what to do with themselves now that their prejudices against you would have to fade. These prejudices, too, that, in fading away, would leave them pale or shaking – which would then be the ultimate confirmation that everything you have ever dared to hope for in your life has now come to pass. And how you would be reserved just a little, or at least until the point when you'd notice they were shaking. At which point you would be kind. So amazingly kind and generous. Warm and friendly and gracious – forgiving them completely, of course, as you imagine it in your fantasy of seeing them again. And so seeing that it was Nathaniel Lord. The shock, the excitement of seeing that it was Nathaniel Lord. But then suddenly recalling, in the hit of an instant, that no matter that Son has told it differently over the years – entirely differently – the bitterness of everything she has said about how biased he'd been towards me – me as the favourite one, me the *favoured one* – and what had supposedly happened after she had been "dumped" from consideration as a result of what she's always called "Lord's massive misjudgement of Woy Woy" – that gallery venture in Woy Woy – that no matter she has claimed he was biased towards me *in every way*, it could well have been the other way round. And so, yes, that is to say: despite all she's been wanting both me and Eileen to believe about what had happened in Woy Woy – *Woy Woy, the Venice of Australia*, as it was supposed to have been thought of as a result of some ancient tourist-seeking venture in the twenties or thirties – this "terrible idea", this *Venice at Woy Woy* that had cost a lot of his money and a lot of her time – her commitment to this gallery project that Nathaniel Lord had "forced" onto her under the guise of doing her a favour. Month after month of travelling up there on his behalf. All those days and weeks of waiting in the gallery for the rich from Killcare or Pearl Beach to "take an interest", and yet all of it coming to an expensive and embarrassing nothing, since nobody in Killcare or Pearl Beach, let alone Woy Woy or Gosford, ever thought it was funny, let alone convincing. Yes, no matter that we've had to believe Sonya when she's said that Nathaniel Lord could "never forgive" her for being the *one to know* that he'd failed in this art and business venture, which, as she's claimed, *never appears in his curricula vitae* – this failure that she carries for him in his place – *she* rather than *he* "copping the flak", as she puts it, for being "totally out of line" with that ignorant and thus highly patronising investment in the Woy Woy gallery project in the first place. No matter that this has been the case for both of us all these years – with our obedient toeing of the Sonya line – I couldn't help thinking that despite the expression of feeling that has always accompanied what she's said – the heightened expression – despite or even because of this high-stakes railing about what is supposed to have happened to her and her art "because of" Nathaniel Lord, it could have well been less of a complaint she was actually making to us – less of a woe – and rather: a claim and a boast. Sonya, that is, boasting to everyone around her and especially to me and Eileen of her particular favour in his eyes, her particular chosenness. Sonya at one time right at the centre of something important, failure or no. And therefore of his belief in her – his enduring belief. And her capacity to hurt him too. My sense, suddenly, then, that Sonya might well have known all along that, despite what had happened in Woy Woy and immediately after Woy Woy, he still believed *she had something in her*, and she wanted us all to know this – especially *me* to know this. And so no matter that her description of what had happened to her back then has always been the accepted version of things, and one that I'd never actually questioned, since I'd always feel chastened as I was hearing it – as if I was far too lucky, undeservedly lucky – no matter that I've always gone along with this way of seeing things with Nathaniel Lord, I had a sense, suddenly, there in Hackney, that I might have got the wrong end of the stick. Because it was not just her highly simplistic description of the Woy Woy gallery venture that should have made me doubt her ostensible view of things – surely he can't have been that stupid – surely – surely not so arrogant either – but rather how she has described everything that has supposedly happened to her ever since – her "exclusion", as she puts it, from the art scene in Sydney. His "vindictive" tendency to exclude her. Or even her accusation that he'd actually *set her up* to take the fall in his place. Yes, no matter she's kept on saying that she has had to bear the brunt of what she calls *a very personal dislike* – and right from the beginning – all the way back to our time in art school, as she claims, and especially since *that show in the final year* – these thoughts she has always vented out loud to all and sundry, as I was thinking in the gallery in Hackney when I saw it was him, indeed – Nathaniel Lord. Him and no one else. That despite all this, I realised that I have always (and also) known that what she was saying about Lord and art school and the venture and everything since was just a gesture, just a claim, because all I could think of, then, was her way of saying these things – her practically beaming as she said them. And also about, how, in fact it was *she alone* who had impressed Nathaniel Lord during that Bodies and Food "happening" at the end of art school – the "sharp delineations" of Sonya's "focus", apparently. Her "extraordinary determination", as I was remembering then, in that gallery in Hackney, when I might have been thinking about me and my own visual art practice instead. Yes, the way that Nathaniel Lord had told me, there in the warehouse space at the end of our final year at art school, about his "encounter" with "our old friend Sonya Hervre" over that wrangling about the chairs for the *happening* – about how it *had* to be those old kindergarten-sized wooden chairs with their raised fire-engine red enamelled dots – those vintage chairs that needed "to be filched" from a school somewhere – one of the "shittier" schools that hadn't "replaced their stock". His way of laughing about Sonya just a little, as he always did about everyone, but this time with such a shine of admiration as well. An incredible shine. "She doesn't beat around", he was saying to me. "Her vision is sharp, unerring". *Telling me everything*, as I was only then starting to realise, in Hackney, in the way that you would describe somebody remarkable to somebody else who wasn't remarkable at all. And that it has never been different from this in fact. That I have always known this. Each of the times I'd gone back to Australia and happened to see one of her shows, I had seen him somewhere there, on the edges of the event, or at least I had sensed his presence, sensed his interest. And so, given how I was feeling about my work on that particular evening in Hackney, it was no wonder that this new perspective on things – on me and Lord and Sonya and me and Lord – had somehow brought it all home to me. That is, what I had done by "taking my eye off the ball", as you might have called it if you'd had any idea of what I was thinking about in my disappointment with the hanging of my pieces – wishing it wasn't me who was there in the gallery, then – or more – wishing that I hadn't agreed to offer these three particular pieces from my "Still Lives" series to Suz and Clem. These pieces that, still – or should I say – *then*, and especially then, looked rather too cloudy – their surfaces thoroughly clouded, in fact filmed over, with some-thing that might only have been the whitish residue of my own anxiety. These pieces that seemed no longer so subtle or layered or surprising, as I had hoped and planned for them to be, but mild and awkward and wrong. Simply wrong. Hoping against hope, then, that all connection be severed between the name this man might have recognised on the paper he had with him there in the gallery and those three awkward pieces that had been suspended seven centimetres out from the wall at their nearest corners (as per my instructions) – those pieces I had, all the same, spent so many months and years developing. How obsessed I had been with those pieces. And continue to be obsessed. So intent on discovering what it was that eluded me about them, and also the way I had been making the pieces smaller – so much smaller than I had before, but also looser and plainer, as if I didn't care at all about what I was doing with the materials. As if I couldn't give a damn that they now looked improvised and also thoroughly unaware of themselves as objects, as "presented images" – which is to say, despite everything I have stated in all my applications for residencies and prizes about the "preciousness of ordinary materiality", about the "simplicity of light". About the "compressed layering of imagery", as I've put it here, there, absolutely everywhere, of "the figure that is caught in the contingency of commercial materialities". This "compressed layering of imagery" etcetera and so forth, and hence my pieces as an unintended undermining – a very physical *anti*-statement – of all this artspeak out of which, nonetheless, I had hoped to make that ten-metre Wall. And so, given how it was with all this fury at myself, at Sonya whom I now envied, at the gallery owners (one of whom I had just started talking to, of course – something about the "try-hard scene in Shoreditch", which I privately preferred to this part of the east), but also this fury at Nathaniel Lord who seemed to be stuck on the connection between the titles of the pieces he was reading on the flier and the artworks themselves. Given all this, how could anyone be surprised at what then transpired between me and Lord, this hunched and irritating man – this shuffling, self-appointed critic-curator who was taking his own sweet time to move his nose between one and the other – the written descriptions and the works themselves? I had the sense that something about my work was puzzling him – something about these three smallish panels – the only ones, you are right, that I had agreed to hand over to Suz and Clem, even though, as you'd kept on pointing out to me, I had "dozens and dozens of these panels". Why hadn't I offered up more of them? you had asked me. Several of the sets? What was I keeping them for? This way that you've long been determined *not* to understand me when I tell you that it didn't seem right that the latest pieces in the series got to be seen by people *yet*. That I didn't feel ready for them to be seen *quite yet*. That, despite all the work I'd been putting into their development – and even showing them in larger groupings – the sheer hard work, as well as the residencies and grants I had been using to help me "mount" this "inquiry into the figure as Still Life" – despite it all, and surely you should know by now how it is with me and these applications, I was still "not there yet" with what I was trying to do with them, and particularly with this project of the Wall. Nowhere near it. And even though – as you've said to me over and over – I've been so success- ful. *I've done so much.*

Despite or because of this anxiety about what I was seeing in Lord – the minutiae of his movements – trying to understand him there in Hackney, I made myself hold on to my memory of the small satisfaction I'd got from making those panels. Yes, the way that, no matter what *he* might have been thinking about me and my pieces, I really had to be thinking about the process of making each of them on the bench in my studio – how once I'd got into the rhythm of working on them I had felt warmed right through with the sense that I was *at last* on the trail of the work that I needed to do. Because how excited I had been. Smaller and smaller the pieces were becoming. Looser and looser. The energy I was discovering in making the work. It was like flying, Teun. Did I ever tell you it was like flying, making the pieces like this? The layering of the translucencies? The layering of images and substances? Actually, I know I didn't tell you then. I feared it would sound stupid. I couldn't bear to hear any of your questions either – any of your usual probing into exactly what I meant. But of this I am sure: as soon as I started taking this so much looser and more daring and intuitive approach to the panels, it began to feel to me as if I were soaring high in the pale of the atmosphere – as if I were just a fat and flightless pigeon that, by accident, had discovered it could fly. "Chuck it in the air" (as they say it here in Oz), and bingo. Flying. In fact, this was when I could at last understand that there were artists who worked in this way, and only in *this* way. Always working with the fat and the wool, as I might have told you at the time, since I remember being struck by how it could be so – "how the art world worked", which was to say how the experience and the work could always be the same, and yet always somehow different as well at the very same time. The exact same shade of limitless, unfathomable blue. Always the same giant floral puppies. Always the mirrors, the ash, the rice, the dry rooted trees that never stop shedding. The shipping containers of asphyxiating nothingness. A physical dark. And yet how it was difficult to keep my confidence in it, Teun – this sense of at last being *on the right track*. In fact, I really don't know how it was that I came up with the idea of the Wall of panels in the first place. A "universe of panels", as I know I've said somewhere, in one of my statements – as if the whole of the universe could be flattened and folded into something that could pre-exist the work itself. And so, on the one hand, the Wall of panels and on the other, the making of what had seemed to me to be the *preparatory* pieces – this always introductory and hence provisional and exciting process of making a thing come to life, if only for the shortest time. And so to Berlin and to Hoorn and to Singapore, Teun. To L.A., to Pusan, to Prague, to Wellington, to Edinburgh. And so the artist – so *effectively* the artist. How proud you were of me, Teun, so happy to see that I was happy. But then – do you remember? – I could also be sickened by what I was doing. How I could be sick – call it chills, call it dread, call it nothing, just a hole, a tunnel that ran its long and insinuating dark through the centre of it all – the whole way through me, from my head, through my heart, through my bowels. And yet, despite this dread, this practically superstitious horror, I kept on with these panels as if only to do something to avoid thinking anymore about the Wall – the ostensible Wall I was supposed to be assembling *in situ*, as I was remembering while I stood there in Hackney watching what looked to be the stubbornness of Lord – the complete incomprehension of Nathaniel Lord. Yes, all of this coming back to me then: my stupefaction with Lord and my shrinking sense of worth as well as my determination to remember something in me that might withstand him. Thinking all this as I worked like an engine in the hallway in dad's place, scraping every bit of the junk that I could find from what was left of the carpet and the rug there – the rags of the rug near the door – realising in my haste, in my utter determination, that this was exactly the sort of work that I had never been able to do for myself before. This picking up of the ephemera, the bits. The bits that usually send me worrying. Even panicking. These leavings of other and better objects, of times in the past that I should rather be *re*-membering in every possible detail and aspect, but clearly wasn't able to. And so the stupid panels, as I like to call them now, I was thinking – first in Hackney, and now again in the house. How galleries had kept on asking me about the "surviving anorexia Wall" but I didn't want to make it – or at least, as I realised, I wasn't ready to make it. How, particularly, I didn't feel like making this horrendously pre-thought-out notion of the Wall as it would be constructed out of some version of my ready-made pieces that they had probably already heard about – perhaps even read about – in the very description of my "Still Lives" project that I'd worded myself. These panels that only ever worked as sweeteners for the larger project – for this other far more *important project*. And so thinking, in this house, in dad's place, about how even the Thinkspate annual showing must have worked like this, at least for Lord – the way Nathaniel Lord must have only *pretended* to want the panels that I had brought out with me this time for his space, or so it had seemed to me afterwards when I'd arrived in Sydney – those panels that had so outraged Sonya Hervre. Those panels that might have been easily overlooked – dismissed by her – had my name not been connected to them. Thinking, too, that he must have only decided to exhibit them at all in this last-minute way because of the Song Dong-*esque* project, which, as he'd written in that piece that went out in that local internet rag – that was *widely shared* and which, as it seems, must have alerted Sonya to the fact that this more ambitious project *was already in the works* – thinking that he had only taken on these smaller pieces because of what they promised in view of that encyclopaedic suburban project, which, as he'd said, "was going to say so much". And so – back then – when I saw that it was indeed *him* standing there in front of the pieces in the Hackney gallery – *inspecting* these pieces, as it so definitely seemed – how awful it had felt because I saw how he was bringing his careful and sceptical attention to these three supposedly important fragments of my "current project", and I could feel I was becoming cold and embarrassed, despite all my attempts to bolster myself – only the Wall thing then in my head, now that my memory of working on the pieces had gone from me – entirely gone. The humiliating obstruction of the Wall. Not the feeling of the flying or the idea – not the futurish, someday-later idea that had been the Wall earlier. Only the pre-known, too-thought-out thing that was to work like Lego pieces on a how-to paper, and so dead as dead and hanging over a fence like a stitched-up carcass. My pieces as carcasses, then, but

94

worse than carcasses. Nylon remnants. Things that were never alive and never to be living. And so it was that I felt in that moment branded all over by the falseness of the cumulative "Wall of anorexia idea", as I'd been describing it in emails sometimes, to my great embarrassment, even to people like Suz and Clem – this sense of how disjunct these three little pieces must have looked alongside everything that Nathaniel Lord might once have noticed about my paintings and drawings at art school – my "quirky pieces", as he had even called the best of the portraits I had been playing around with in the earlier years, before the final show. And then the "courage and authenticity" of our "happening" at art school – that so very awkward event, which, nonetheless, seemed to elevate me – indeed all of us – somewhere brilliant. Somewhere *going far*. This performance with our "*real* bodies", as everyone kept describing it – those images we had made of ourselves that had "knocked the socks off all those fusty modernists", as Lord had even called the other teachers at the time. His own associates. How cutting he had been. The way that he had laughed as he described the obscure obsessions and preferences of one, the "anally attentive" style of another – "always in black". The cramped and precious sort of elegant style that, as I gathered, he hated with a passion and with a sense of justified rightness. This sense, at the time, I'd have of him being above, and removed, and hence never wrong – never wasting any time on irrelevant panderings to irrelevant standards. So definitely on the good and authentic side of an aesthetic (and ethical) shoreline of art. And so it was that this sensitivity I still apparently had when I was near him regarding everything I had done in my life until this point – and especially everything I imagined him seeing that I'd done – that this sensitivity had wound into what I was saying to the owner Clem about the art scene in Shoreditch. This rant about some artists that "really annoyed me". Their work that was so "naff". Their arch use of seventies cliché that had been "done to death". On and on about the work of these artists that had merely come to the surface of my mind, as it seemed, when I was trying to prepare myself for the moment when Nathaniel Lord would turn around to see that it was indeed *I* who had made the artworks he was standing in front of, and so first – as I imagined it – having to hear me out about that "scene" I was trying to describe to Clem. That scene in Shoreditch that I envied, in fact, rather than despised. How even thinking about these artists – and "the horrible mementoes from my horrible childhood that they clearly didn't understand" – was intended, from the first, to prepare me to catch the eye of my old art school mentor as he turned from where he was standing near my panels, to come this way and engage with me – very possibly, to get another drink from the table, or else to look at the images that were next in sequence on the list in the catalogue – the last in line. This rant of mine that could only have been intended to make me all the readier to look straight back at him the very second he looked to appraise whether I was indeed as "quirky" as he appeared to have thought back then "in the day". A quirky and original kind of thinker. Or indeed the kind of "discerning artist" he (as I'd imagined) always admired.

What a relief it had been to sit in the car on the way home after the opening – after my anxious reactions to Nathaniel Lord, and everything I had done and said after noticing he was there. What a relief, then, to have had dad to point to – to have been able to talk to you about dad and about how "everything loses meaning when you are trying to understand that someone close to you has died". To talk to you about how bad I had been feeling that I had made it "such a priority" to show up to the opening of this "frankly, pathetic" show instead of making sure I was already back in Sydney "with the family". So much easier to say all of this than to admit to anything else. It also didn't help to remember, in the car, that in the weeks leading up to the show, I had heard you going on and on to our friends and basically to anyone that you talked to about how pleased I had been to be included in this "exciting" call-out, and "after such a time of not much happening" for me – how very pleased to be having these three small pieces that I had been working on for several years – and working on "far too much", as you had observed – these three small pieces in a show like this with "all those other up and coming artists". I had already heard you describe me thus to our friends. And I have told you, too, many times, that I didn't have the heart to disagree with you in front of them. How mean and petty I would have seemed if I had said that this "cutting-edge" exhibition, as you'd kept on calling it, was just another way of saying how so very *un*established were the artists represented, so very *un*established the crowd.

Because you see, Teun, when I am not standing still and stunned, not knowing why it is that I cannot do the simplest things that other people can do – when I am not completely appalled and ashamed, or stuck and confounded about how even to begin to handle the filth and the mess that surrounds me always (yes, even in London, I know that I'm mired – completely mired). When I am not just stuck, I know that I can be filled with such an immensity of feeling that the room, the world, becomes an extension of my mind – an extension of my mood (the kind of feeling that would have me stride – reckless and unprepared – towards the peak of Everest, or that would save all the orphans of Cambodia with a *perfect plan*). This feeling that is so private, so strange. Such a strange kind of madness – a fierce and deluded machine – but nonetheless a feeling or conviction I once thought Nathaniel Lord had actually admired in me. Or at least back then, when I had decided to go ahead with that Bodies and Food "happening" at art school, despite everything that had seemed so wrong about it. The dread that I was soaking in at the time – the anger, the bitterness (from Sonya and Eileen) – my sense that I shouldn't be listening to Lord when he said I needed to ignore them. This heady risk I was taking with it all. Because at least he had noted and approved of my "energy", as he'd called it – my "distinctive energy". And perhaps this was what I had understood, too, as soon as I realised in Hackney that he was indeed this person I remembered – this one-time mentor – this *renaissance man of Sydney*, Nathaniel Lord. Yes, this figure that I might otherwise have taken for a lugubrious and homeless man. Either an eccentric peer with his too-comfortable jacket – a contemporary version of a left-wing tweed – or something just risen from dirt-ringed rags in the street outside. One extreme or the other. This need, then, to summon inside me some glowing remnant of that "distinctive energy" for this shrivelled-down man and his buckling, plastic cup of black blood wine – for this man with his gawping neck and his way of sniffing and clearing his throat as if he were continually signalling to someone or other that he were about to deliver a weighty thought, or rather, as if, with the whole of this elaborate, complete and intense attention he gave to a work – an exaggerated version of this kind of attention – he was in fact only aping and mocking the lot of us there.

I know I shouldn't have felt so afraid of him – so spooked by the attention of this so much older and smaller Nathaniel Lord than I might ever have imagined him being – this Nathaniel Lord who had always seemed to take his view of what he saw as the *only* view of something – who liked to see himself, as if from afar, as the one attentive person in a crowd of fools. How important it had been to know him back then, I was telling myself even as I was making a fool of myself to Clem. This way that I was trying to remember how firmly he had once believed in me – and also in Sonya – especially in Sonya – and even in Eileen. Of course, we had been lazy too. At least *I* had been lazy. And yet his was the sort of attention that stirred me – that seemed to get me moving, scrambling, towards the goal or dream that I had always hoped to be moving towards, and hence seemed to prompt me to take myself much more seriously as an *artist* – to become something more than the hopeless case that I'd always felt myself to be in the eyes of the other teachers, for whom my tentative artworks, alongside my awkward body – my clearly very anxious body – my frankly thin and still *emaciated* body with its too-large head, its obsessive eyes – had made me – indeed made the three of us – into that conglomerate of "sicko girls", as I had overheard one of the teachers calling us. Thus it was that Nathaniel Lord had been the only teacher to take us seriously. The three of us. The only one to be – or at least to appear to be the one who was curious about what we thought or about what we did. This way that Nathaniel Lord, I was thinking – yes, forcing myself to think – had been the only one in the entire staff at art school to engage with the idea of the "happening" that was to save our skins after the disaster of the flood that had destroyed most of our works earlier in the year. Nathaniel Lord alone of all the teachers to be curious enough to ask some questions – to become provocative even – pushing me – and then, later, the three of us – to develop what we had only half thought through with the food and not even half thought through with our bodies. He alone seeing something in our projected performance that wasn't just, as one teacher had put it, "a weird kind of Greenaway rip-off". Yes, if it wasn't for Nathaniel Lord – as I remember thinking in some concentrated way even as I was still saying all that nonsense to Clem about the artists in the scene in Shoreditch – if it wasn't for him, I wouldn't have had any career worth speaking of now. I could well have stopped making art altogether. This "feisty red head", as he used to be, who – out of all the teachers there in art school – had been the only one to believe in us, and what we could do, at a time that mattered so much to us all – who pushed us in such a way that we might have, just as easily, made colossal fools out of ourselves as not. Who might, rather, have been hoping we'd fail in a spectacular manner – and so much so that he would have been able to laugh at us alongside everyone else who would have been laughing at us already. And so of course it was at this moment of strange confusion in my thinking that Nathaniel Lord had come up to me with that familiar and warm but still highly ironic grin of his – that way of greeting me as if it hadn't been so many years since last he saw me. The way he had laughed, too, at *how much I had changed*: "Wearing so many more clothes" than the last time "we'd been in the same room". An infectious laughter. And suddenly it didn't matter that I had been saying such rubbish to Clem about the Shoreditch scene, or indeed that he might have – long ago – wanted Eileen, Son, and I to implode in a public way, because the minute he introduced himself to Clem as Nathaniel Lord of Thinkspate Galleries in Sydney and then went on to tell her how "fascinated" he had always been with the persistence of my interest in the figure and its obsessions, the horizon cleared from here to the English Channel. This way he was now calling everything I had done back then, "the figure and its obsessions". And so, for a while, or at least until his questions started to get too close to things – too probingly close – I could feel that I had just been lifted a little into the air by the thoughts of

99

Lord, the benevolent attention of Nathaniel Lord. These thoughts that I, nonetheless, was compelled to direct *away* from the Wall the very second I had been drawn by him to offer it up. Yes, *completely away*. This benevolent attention, which I actually thought, in the minutes and hours that followed, I had squandered with my bizarre and uncalled-for reference to a project I was working on "then" *in the mode of the Chinese conceptual artist Song Dong*.

How bitter I was in the car that evening. It's not so easy, you had said to me, losing a dad.

And yet, later that evening, the message that Lord left on my mobile about meeting up "as soon as possible" so that he could "probe me more about the *Chatswood Song Dong project*", which now could only be the following morning – that teasing tone, and then the laugh – the kind of laughter with which you get to imagine, if only for a second, that you are somehow on intimate and inclusive terms – no longer being laughed *at* by the laughter he is offering but rather being sheltered inside it, coddled by the laughter – as if the two of you were the only ones on the entire globe of the world who were sitting inside it – this message frightened me even as it soothed. So when I returned the call early the next morning, I tried to stop myself from showing Nathaniel Lord how disconcerted I had been to hear that he wanted to meet with me about "the project" – playing the *cool professional*, I told myself when I pressed in his number to call him back. Playing the sort of person who is always getting asked so many questions that one more question will not faze her, will not fell her to the ground. And so that teasing, too, that followed on the phone when he said how it would be much more "seemly" for us to meet up at the café at the Tate – the Tate Modern of course (again the laughter). He wanted to hear a bit more about what I was planning to do by bringing what Song Dong had developed – "the clarity of his approach" – to the problem of my father, and so to my parents, in the "very different context of *suburban Sydney*".

And, yes – of course, as I remember thinking – I should have known it – how Nathaniel Lord always loved this word "suburban" – this enchanting word "suburban", I was even thinking as I walked to the Tube on my way to our meeting that day after the opening, and with such a smile on my face that it soon felt sore. Coming from anybody else, I had been thinking then, "suburban" would have been an *anti*-art word. A killing-all-art word. But from Nathaniel Lord, it was the sweetest of descriptors. How heavenly, how perfect, to find yourself smack bang at the centre of the gaze of your old art school mentor from Sydney, I was telling myself as I was walking along Roman Road, no matter that it felt ridiculous – even appallingly ridiculous – to be thinking in this way. Because this was when I began to feel that there might have been something special, almost magically perfect, in the notion of this *Song Dong approach* to the stuff in dad's house – something that had done its special sure work for me even before I had realised it, and even though I had said (as I'd thought) the very *wrong thing* by telling Lord about it in Hackney when I did. *Done its work*, as if the saying of this otherwise random bit of stupidity had been a spell, a charm, a queer-looking key that I hadn't been able to recognise for the magic object that it was – that I might have tossed away. Because it seemed that even if I hadn't been *consciously* planning such a project with the leavings of everything that was so difficult about my family and the house, a much better part of me – some far less logical, and so more intuitive, more empathetic and more *connected* part of me – had been doing all this planning about it nonetheless, and had even known that such a project would be able to do what my "Still Lives" panels could never do (apparently). That even the Wall could never do (apparently). Since a show on this scale – such a *selflessly generous scale* – was far more likely to make sense of everything in my life that I had, thus far, not been able to understand. Yes, how this approach (via Song Dong) had seemed to be so right, so ethical, so exactly on the nail, as it were, for solving all my problems – all my artistic problems, as much as my personal problems, with my family and the house. How it seemed to *connect* with everything that had been lying underneath every one of my thoughts about dad and mum and the life I'd had there with them – with all of my thoughts about "everything I came from", as I have kept on calling it over the years. All the conversations with you, too – even though, when I told you about my "plans for the house" after I'd got home from talking to Lord at the Tate Modern – or at least when *you* got home – you also asked those other sorts of questions, such as what are you going to do if you can't get hold of Angus? And: shouldn't *he* have a say in all this? Do you even think it's realistic, you'd then asked after I'd told you *everything* – your asking and asking, just to check that – really – it had been my idea – and only my idea – *all along*. That I wasn't simply allowing Nathaniel Lord to set me onto something that was more "his sort of thing" than *my* "sort of thing" (as you kept on calling it).

In fact, as I was clearing out the hallway in dad's place, I kept thinking about how, on my way to that meeting with Nathaniel Lord at the café at the Tate Modern, all I'd been thinking about was my *agency*. Obsessed with my *agency*. I really wasn't thinking about the project *per se* but how I would frame it, or continue to frame it. I remember that I had been thinking about how it would be necessary to be clear and definite about my limitations, and hence my differences, vis-à-vis the *Waste Not* project of the artist Song Dong – about how I would describe what my own approach would involve, which is to say how the house and the circumstances in Sydney were "different". The cultural context "entirely different". Because I knew that it was going to be crucially important to at least *seem* to limit my hubris, Teun, and yet also appear to be strong as well. As strong as I could: steady, strong. Nathaniel Lord was late for the meeting, of course, more than thirty minutes late. And then there was all the fussing about where he and I should sit. Not with my back to the doorway, he had said the minute he approached where I was already sitting waiting for him near the window glass. It's "just a masculine anxiety thing", he had said with that goofy laugh of his, which somehow made it all the easier to describe what I would do with the Chatswood house and "the effects" of my dad – to tell him (albeit a little too hastily) about how it could "in no way approach" what Song Dong had done with what I called "the residue of political upheaval and the singular personal tragedy of his mother" – and "hence no such clarity and order", I had added as well – since what I would be dealing with would be the confusion and "useless remnants" of *tragedies whose pained and nodal moments continued to elude me* – upheavals so "domestic", as I was saying in the language that seemed to emerge specifically for the ears of Nathaniel Lord – upheavals that could only be guessed at in the very "pathos and scope" of the "myriad collections" I was going to make. And that I would have to work on it all in a far more intuitive way. How easily the words were turning themselves out of me, then, as if it had been the *words* doing the talking – the very perfection of this serendipitous thought about Song Dong – this serendipitous approach to using his ideas – that was doing the talking instead of me. And of course, the seriousness of my attempt to make sure, as it might well have seemed, that I was "doing the best" by my father and his house and his memory. "Doing the best" by everyone concerned in everything that I said. Even by Song Dong, and his considerable legacy in the international art world. Even by that. Yes, how I played up to what I'd guessed in that moment in the Tate Modern Café to be the rapt expectations of Nathaniel Lord. How I managed to handfeed him the most brilliant and generous thoughts and impressions, which, of course, were not really mine to pass on at all.

So much effort to convince Nathaniel Lord, I was thinking as I stood for a while near the newly cleared entrance to the doorway of the lounge room where dad and Angus had spent so much time during my last visit to Sydney – this entrance, which was nonetheless clogged by an impossible tower of boxes and magazines and plastic bags. So much effort to say – to insist on saying – how indebted I was going to be to Song Dong, *of course*. That it would be a kind of homage. A necessary homage. Indeed, also saying how I was "*well aware*" that the problems of suburban Sydney in the sixties and seventies did not compare "at all" to the problems of existence during the Cultural Revolution in the People's Republic. How the trumped-up privations and anxieties here were "nothing" to the "*real* ones there". Ah, this way I worked so hard in the café with Nathaniel Lord – sitting side on, as we were, to the river – side on to the city and everything there – working so hard to make sure that, in spite of how it must have looked to Nathaniel

Lord at the Hackney show, I had indeed become a *real* and exciting and serious and *highly engaged* artist during my several decades working, as I hoped he'd have read in a statement on my Weebly site, "with the self and its difficulties in the ever-changing image-scape of the media" on the other side of the world.

I pulled the boxes of newspapers and bags whose only burden seemed to come from the expanded fibres and months of waiting, probably, in the doorway like this, for a decision to be made about their fate – these nothingy boxes that rasped and caught as I pulled them across the balding bristles on the rods of the front doormat, which as I could see was the exact same door-mat that dad had always kept on the porch to rub his old grease-smeared boots on before coming into the house after he'd been working on the car. I pulled out the boxes. Even pushed them so that they bounced and tipped down the steps any-old-how onto the path and the garden, spilling their papery and rusty contents all over the lawn. All this shit in the garden, I imagined saying to you then. *You should see all the shit in the garden.* Yes, so much effort to impress that old mentor of mine, Nathaniel Lord – a massive effort, which, surprisingly, had come very naturally to me as I sat on the chair with my back to the door in that café at the Tate Modern – on the chair he had asked to swap with me – sitting where he had got me to move after the reference to his "masculine anxiety", and then leaning towards him in such a way that I might have been listening *so enthusiastically* to everything he was saying. All this listening. Playing the serious contemporary artist for the benefit of this man who happened to have Lord as his name, with the whole of me funnelled into this high-stakes game of convincing Nathaniel Lord – trying to impress the very person who, for all I knew (since I had only thought to google his name in the seconds before he arrived), might have become little more than an *ex* art history teacher and academic, an *ex* small gallery owner. A no one from Australia with no influence at all.

I remember, as I was listening to him talk in the café at the gallery on the Thames, that I was beginning to savour how my world was now breath-ing outwards, through the glass, to the river, to the remote-looking buildings on the shore beyond – that I was becoming – at last – the kind of thought-ful, adventurous, pedantic, and *supra-quirky* artist that I might have hoped to become when I quit Australia for the more "serious half" of the world, as I had once described it for you, Teun. Becoming the significant and important artist that I had risked my all to become, rather than one who, instead, only runs away from everything she does or tries to do – always running – working by avoiding and running. Always running a long way away. Yes, because even then in the café at the Tate Modern I also knew that what I was saying to Nathaniel Lord was nothing but a sham. Everything I was saying or doing with this "listening" of mine was concocted. All of it concocted. This terrible sense that I was piling one lie on top of another – one confounding concoction – a sandwich of concoctions – over and over, and in a tower that was growing higher and higher the longer it went on. And yet it had also felt good to be participating in this grand sort of sham, because it *seemed to be working.* After all, I was feeling so generous and good as I was talking and listening, and so perhaps – as I might have hoped – I was *really becoming* the very thing I was imagining myself to be. *Making myself out to be.* What an artist, Nathaniel Lord might have been thinking (as *I* had been thinking in part) – what a "generous take" she has on it all. And so it was in this hope that I might really have become – only now and *at long, long last* – the passionate, humane, focussed and *extraordinarily inventive* artist that I had hoped to become when I moved to London only eighteen months after finishing art school in Sydney (even though I was still, as my mother had put it in a letter afterwards, nothing but "skin and bone"). Only now feeling that I had arrived into my *self* as the artist I had always hoped to become: one that I could *feel* was thriving and "growing", as everyone puts it. Yes, as you can see, no matter that it was so much of a performance for Lord – everything I was saying and evoking in every move that I made (in the way, for instance, I leaned for a moment with my chin on the heel of my hand), it was also, I could see at the very same time, an apparently authentic bringing forth for him of all that had been coiled in me since the year I had gone to London with my "anorexic mindset", as I think Sonya had called it that time I visited her in Casino many years later, when we at last got to talk about "things that mattered" – Sonya, who had told me she was "past all that shit" in the email she sent me afterwards, and "*couldn't* I see it" – how it was "bleeding obvious" – the missive that followed the email that *I* had sent *her* in an effort to explain what I thought had gone wrong during that visit – my attempts to suggest that we both had a "problem". That the two of us still might have been mired in our problems – our supposedly (post)-anorexia problems. And yet, really, I was thinking as I pulled more and more of the boxes and papers out through the doorway from the lounge room where I got a glimpse, as I moved, of the old green armchair that dad used to sit in – basically to sink in, towards the ratty old carpet on the floor. Really, it seemed to me then, in the house, that I must have known from the moment I said it, even in that gallery in Hackney, that Lord would *definitely* pick up on what I had said about the work of Song Dong, the celebrated Chinese artist, as an "inspiration" for the work I'd supposedly already planned to make for myself. Which meant that right from the beginning I was involved in an artifice – a deliberate and devious artifice. After all, I had managed to convince Lord, and then myself, and so why not you later as well – and after that everyone else – that just as Song Dong was the artist that had proved it was possible to ingest and so transform – in its entirety – the whole of the material amassing of his traumatised mother, my description of it all could ingest and transform any doubts or gaps that *you* might still have about it? I had even "realised", I told you (as I remember), that an "Antipodean" and "post-colonial version" of something very similar was the "one specific factor that my work was needing" – admittedly, a "far more ordinary and humble version of the approach", I had said – to you, and probably to Lord as well, in an effort to be, or at least to *seem* to be, ordinary and humble about such a claim. An outlandish claim. Song Dong's work being the *stuff,* I had said, *of universal pain and anxiety.* Yes, trying to make it clear that I realised that all of us are landed with the inheritance of this pain and anxiety from the experiences of the ones who have formed us – our minds, our selves as well as our bodies – in our earliest years. Telling you, in case you'd forgotten (I'd said as well), that the inspiration for all of this was the artist whose show had "so moved me" when I'd seen it in The Curve at the Barbican. Each of the objects, I had said – the sad, battered histories of the brushes, the jars, the pens, the shoes. The pathos of their incredible order and profusion. Everything kept and arranged and so beautifully displayed. My father's place is like this *as you know*, I am sure I had even said to you with the very same tone that I had said it to Nathaniel Lord in the café at the Tate Modern – at least the contents of the house. And since mum died, it has become all the more "byzantine", all the more "excessive": dad then distributing the objects everywhere – everywhere imaginable, I remember adding most suggestively if not quite truthfully, since I had known that dad had always done this, and that it had *always* been byzantine, always been excessive, or so I also liked to think, considering that I only had Angus's word for how the house and its contents had changed since I last was there. Dad's problem never having been one of accumulating objects *per se*, I remember thinking even then, but without initially wanting to say so to either you or Nathaniel Lord. He was never so much drawn to accumulating individual objects, I was thinking again in the house in Chatswood, at the doorway to the lounge room where, past the back of dad's old green velvet chair, I had a glimpse of a mound of something that might have been clothing or layers of carpet underlay, and also of the familiar faux-wooden shell of his old nineteen-eighties television set. Not so much an obsession with accumulating individual objects, then, but rather with everything those objects connected to – everything they held between them and which joined them together. The remnants of my father's projects. All of his unfinished projects – his manifold theories – the haze of his ideas. Not the objects but the theories, I was thinking once more, as I remembered what I had said to you, then in London, now that I was pulling more of these boxes and oddments past the doorway of the lounge room, and so out from that room as well. So that I might at last get to see the whole of the room and its furniture that had once been so familiar to me – this room that mum had once kept as clean and orderly as she could for "visitors". Dad never stockpiled objects for their own sakes, for themselves, I was remembering saying to both you and Lord, because he was far too busy stockpiling his theories that, perhaps, might have needed all of these boxes into which he could store what he would have called his "reams of evidence" – dad having always had so many "mountains of evidence" for his theories, I was remembering – some of it from books, although much of it, too, from newspapers and the odd torn-out pages of *Time* magazines or those shiny pamphlets that sit in their cages out the front of health food shops in shopping centres. This evidence that was everywhere, all over his study and all over the house, since dad hadn't been allowed (by mum) to have "enough filing cabinets", as he used to complain. This way that she was always "interfering" with his projects, as I would constantly hear from him – these projects of his that were always in process, always "in train". And yet so much of its material substance was, even then – at the time – all yellowed and torn and in a state of disintegrating chaos, I was thinking as I brought to mind some of the earlier signs of this chaos – the piles, at the ends of the kitchen table and on the floor, of many, many weeks, if not months, of newspapers, each of them with the numbers noted of which pages had yet to have an article clipped from it *and filed away*. Some labelled by mum, of course, but so many more by dad's much heavier and shakier hand. Whatever the conflict between mum and dad about the state of the house, I was remembering, there was never any conflict about the need to accumulate newspapers, and to bore through the centre of them, in a very great effort to find out *why* and *how*.

Right then, I could see that it was addictive thinking about the problem of the house. It is still addictive. How easy, in fact, it had been to talk about "everything that I feared" about the house as I looked across at the Thames with Nathaniel Lord – where this *everything* I described for him was a profusion of "objects" which, as such, was destined to fascinate the man, since hadn't he always been interested in "the placement of objects" – objects and their "vernaculars", as I remembered him saying all those years ago in one of the courses he taught at art school – the "encyclopaedic" attraction of "collections of objects"? How very easily, then, did I describe what I remembered in dad's study at the other end of the house to be the vast collections of rulers in every length and material – Bakelite, plastic, wood, steel – as well as the satisfyingly disparate collections of books that dad had labelled with the numbers and letters of a Dewey decimal system on tiny rectangles of taped paper – rectangles that had been written on with what would have been one of those disposable green-bodied Pentel pens that, itself, would have been similarly labelled with the date that it was last refilled with ink. The more I talked about such details to Lord, and of the care that dad had always taken to make sure that it worked – his meticulous system – the surer I felt that this was a project that *had* to be made "in honour of dad". It was easy to talk about the house as I had imagined it then – and increasingly through Nathaniel Lord's eyes – as a "powerfully ordinary example", or so he was later to state in an email confirmation of what we discussed in our meeting at the Tate – of this installation that would "stage a post-war manifestation of twentieth- and twenty-first-century anxiety on a suburban Australian scale". Yes, how easy it had been to talk about the process of solving the problem of the house through the "reinventive practices of art". Of course, I was never going to be able to negotiate with dad in the way that Song Dong had negotiated with his own mother. I could also see that it was too late to be thinking in any more detail about my *own* thoughts on any of this – any of my more genuine thoughts on dad and the house. But how smoothly (I imagined) the whole of the leavings of my family could be settled and contained and boxed and solved as if the mass of what we were talking about were something that was completely separate from me in fact. As if the seventeen thousand kilometres between the leavings and me had already eased the essential problems with the project, or even guaranteed the success of this apparently "provocative and engaging" installation that was going to be assembled in the foyer of Lord's new Eveleigh art space, which was "crying out" for a show on a scale like this.

So glad, then, that I had managed it so that it was Nathaniel Lord, and not me, who had been asking about the exhibition – the exhibition that only *I* could provide for *him*. This way that it had all worked out so that he was keen to be the one to host it. That he had already determined it would be assembled in the broad industrial foyer of his Thinkspate Galleries in Eveleigh as soon as the 2020 project of the "disintegrating wheat-belt" sculpture (a sculpture that celebrated the "enduring riches of the Australian rural cultural imaginary") had run its course. This way, too, that in stating what I had about the projected installation, I seemed to have miraculously solved every one of my difficulties with home and family through the thoroughly ethical and sensitive engagement that is always being promised in the processes of art. And so this transformation of the contents of dad's place into an exhibition – this "brilliantly provocative" idea, as Nathaniel Lord kept calling it. *An Antipodean and appropriately suburban version of Song Dong's approach to connective practice. This powerfully ordinary statement of post-war twentieth- and twenty-first-century anxiety.* How Nathaniel Lord's wide-flecked nose had gone pink and even pinker as he received what I said about this Song Dong treatment of the family house in Chatswood. How quickly he had been stirred to articulate his "own ideas" about the show as well – ideas that he fed to me as we sat in the café at the Tate Modern, looking out at the city of London as well as the river – the two of us playing the artist and the far-seeing mentor. That old, old tale. The way his eyes had hung heavy, even halfway shut, as if he were already being sated with the sort of pleasure that only *I* could have brought to him – to this eminent and thoughtful associate from the other side of the world. In fact, after a while he told me that he had been "*so* pleased" to have come across that show in Hackney – glad to have seen those "distinctive little pieces" in the corner, which he might not have spotted at all if it hadn't been his wont to comb every inch of a gallery. There are always "gems" in the "darkest of corners", he so satisfyingly said. If I had anything similar, he then added, I could send it over to him for his upcoming annual show. Registered post. Or bring it over with me in the plane, he said, when he heard I was flying to Australia anyway – in fact the very next day – since it was important to get a piece or two in front of "the punters" in order "to start it all happening".

But he knew the pieces wouldn't sell, he then told me quickly, and with a certainty that was so strong and so quietly sure, that I went cold inside. He said that it was "really interesting" that I was still obsessed with the pathos of the empty figure, and he was smiling as he said this to me. Smiling, and even sly. As if he had always known something important about me that, in all these years, I hadn't known properly or in sufficient detail for myself.

I can't help remembering as I write all this down here in this document, that when I first told you, Teun, about my supposed plan to "salvage something of my life in Australia" through the "lens" of Song Dong, there was something in your response that unsettled me as well. It was the way you had followed me around the flat with your questions that were probably only attempts to make sure I hadn't been talked into this idea by "that strange old teacher" I'd had in Australia, as you called him – to make sure that it was *my* idea and had only ever been mine. And so, in order to reassure you that this idea that might have seemed to have arrived from nowhere had actually been something that *I* had been thinking about *for a good long while*, I began my attempt to convince you that this was an extremely important idea for me – that in fact it had been "slowly simmering inside me" since the Barbican show. *At least since then.* And so the effort I made in this attempt to make you see that something of the beginnings of it dated at least from the time I had visited Sydney *before* my mother's death – that is, well before I had seen what I saw at the Barbican with Arijit. How I worked very hard for you to be able to accept that this was true – that this idea for the Song Dong project was my own – my own highly engaged and authentic idea. But then the minute you had given in and, at last, seemed to believe me – perhaps even the minute I managed to convince myself – my whole feeling about the project changed, and as soon as I heard you describing to our neighbours what it was that I was now going back to do in Sydney – as soon as I heard you saying all this as we were stepping out the front of our place onto Roman Road early the next morning with my luggage – it became difficult not to rise up in revolt against everything you said. So difficult not to try to defend what I thought I was doing from the strange inflections you had brought to what you were saying about my "interesting plans" for the Sydney house. And yet on what grounds did I have to push against it when it had been *me* who had fed you the lies in the first place? *Me* who had forced you to say such crap? Because, of course, I couldn't let on to you, at the time, anything about the immensity of what I was fearing about the house – anything that suggested, too, that the Song Dong idea might have been invented, simply, to avert something else. Because this place, this house, isn't at all dead yet, I've been thinking as I write all this here. There's no afterwards time to make work from – no afterwards time in which everything is already safe and packaged and waiting. In fact, I can see that nothing here in this house is just an object that is waiting for me to subject it to *another* order of being. Everything is still alive and dangerous. Yes, everything here in this house is tainted with its own aliveness, even now that all of it has gone. And I can recognise that I was forced to see this for myself even when I circled the outside of the house at the very beginning – as soon as I got here – wondering how on earth I was going to get in closer to it, since the earth, the fence, the vines, the grey-paned windows, the walls themselves seemed to have turned their backs on me. When I was forced to think, too, for the very first time perhaps, about how it must have been for dad that day when he was found raving and feverish all alone on the scuffed-dry lawn out the front of the house – moving and muttering and practically naked, as I had learned from someone, probably Angus.

So instead of telling you, then, about how I had concocted the idea of the Song Dong take on my father's house for the very same art school mentor I should rather have avoided given the way that, all those years ago, he had jumped too eagerly onto the idea I had brought to him after the flooding in Gibbens Street in Camperdown. Instead of owning up to the confusion of my responses to this supposed mentor given his role in that notorious work that it was still too embarrassing to remember – embarrassing and yet thrilling (what a break it had afforded me in the art world: me, Eileen and Sonya, too – how I'd had to be brave, uncaring – they, too, brave and uncaring, with this work that might have allowed us to develop what we were only then beginning to recognise in ourselves: this sense of what it actually felt like to exist in anorexic bodies, in anorexic minds; this tiny and precious glimpse of something that was soon made, of course, to give way to *his* more articulate take on it all). Yes, instead of admitting to any of this, I had said to you, before I left Australia, that it felt *so right* to be making this work for Nathaniel Lord's new art gallery space in Eveleigh in Sydney – because (as I said) I had at last understood what it might be possible to *do* with the leavings of the most difficult period of my life in a properly *non*-European, and so, completely *Antipodean* context. Which meant that despite everything you had said to me earlier, immediately after you heard that dad had died and that the solicitor was wanting to talk to me about what to do about the house – despite what you had explicitly said about what you would do if you were *in my shoes* with such a house as you remembered it when you'd come with me to Australia "that time" – you had come all the way around from your natural tendency to urge a more practical and drastic solution to the problem of the house. A "healthy" solution, as you'd even called it. Which was to say that you, Teun, had turned one hundred and eighty degrees around from your otherwise clear sort of *un*sentimental view on it all – until you became, instead, not only a whole lot less negative about this clearly impractical idea of the Song Dong approach to the house, but also entirely supportive of my plans to tackle the house in the way that I'd said I would. You, Teun, becoming then – and as I might have predicted if it really *had* been my own idea – my *own* authentic idea – becoming from this point onwards my most generous and avid supporter for this "ambitious plan", as you described it to our shop owning neighbours below our flat in Roman Road.

What a load of shit, I caught myself saying out loud in dad's place on the morning I was pulling the whole thing apart. I went back into the hall to take out more and more of the scurrilous leavings of paperclips and pens and sticks and flyers and letters (still not opened) and bottle tops and the dusty shells of plastic packaging – so much stiff, clear packaging, as if dad had been constantly buying the sorts of small electrical devices that might be connecting one object to another – all of them connected – all over the house. And what a relief not to be thinking of having to file it all, to collect it all, I was thinking, even though I was also beginning to see how I might have proceeded with the work on it all the same – now that the hallway had some space in the centre of it. Now that so many bags and boxes had gone. How I might have begun to make all the many and necessary micro-collections that I would then have needed to sort and categorise and store. But of course, as I was telling myself too: I have said what I've said in that email to Lord – telling myself over and over as I bent down to pull at a twisted rug that had been left, rubbery black-side up under a pile of heavy, weighted cloth that could have been curtains, and which then unfolded – all of a sudden, as soon as I pulled on it – to reveal a small caked cargo of dried-out faeces or perhaps only mud. The whole of it trailing in a flaking, stinking mess across to the porch and down the stairs, and then flung onto the gargantuan heap of things I'd piled on the lawn. I have sent that email, I was thinking then. And since that email: nothing. Nothing at all. Perhaps I was cruel to have sent it to Lord when I did – sending it only days after the "social media storm" that followed Sonya's "intervention" at the Wharf. But, really, *this* is how to do it, I was telling myself, too. It's the only way. Trying to reassure myself that it had been necessary to write to Nathaniel Lord at such a time. *Even at such a time.* When I wrote to thank him "for his enthusiastic support" and to state in unambiguous terms that, despite the arrangements we had already made – everything we had planned – it was best for everybody that the Song Dong-*esque* project "should no longer go ahead".

I need to remind you now that, until that sharp turnaround in your thinking about it, you, Teun, had been onto me, rather, about "getting it all sorted". And then there were all of your suggestions, your generous attempts to help – yes, every one of your reminders about making the call to get a skip as soon as I arrived in the country. Since it didn't take a minute, you'd said to me over and over. You're always making things excessively hard for yourself. What's wrong with getting help? My god. If you don't feel like getting one of those sorting companies to help you, you should at least get a skip. Because, until I had managed to convince you, Teun, that this "more empathetic" approach – this Song Dong approach – was the one I was set upon – that it *hadn't* been Lord's idea at all, but only mine – and thus that it had been me and me alone who had proposed *the Song Dong solution*, as you also came to call what it was that I was about to do for the house. Until I'd convinced you, finally (as I thought), that what I was planning to do was going to be a complete answer, which was to say an "ethical and aesthetic" solution, to everything about my life and the lives of my family that had overwhelmed me in the past – until this decisive moment, all of our discussions about what I was going to do when I got to Sydney had been about how difficult it was going to be to "deal with the house" now that Angus had definitely scooted. That and the way that a contracting business or at least a skip would be necessary, as you said, *the minute I arrived*. Not that they were really discussions, I will admit now, in this document I'm preparing for you to read. They weren't discussions, I remember. Because, while you were speaking, and hence while you were saying what you were saying, I hadn't said a thing, or at least nothing other than to assert that contractors were *unfeeling people* – that *they wouldn't know what to keep and what to throw* – these notions I had grabbed hold of from somewhere – so sure I had been – that anyone who "sorted out" houses professionally would have to be a *cold* kind of person. *Cold and hard*. Which meant that all of this only came to a halt when at last I'd committed to doing the very thing that was, earlier, out of the question – when, after weeks of inexplicable prevarications with Nathaniel Lord, who had wanted my commitment "in writing" if he were going to arrange the space and the hiring and storage of a shipping container for my projected exhibition of "the contents of the Chatswood house" in 2020 – after all of this, and less than a day after I'd returned from the beginnings of that trip to Mudgee to track down Eileen for Max – "just to see if she was there" (that trip that was cut very short when Max had rung with the news of the accident – when I'd had to say I was "extremely sorry" to hear what had happened – that I would return the car, and put the keys where they would be, as he said, "safe" in the letter-box – how stunned I had been – with the image of the accident, especially, even though I hadn't been there for it – the notion of the accident. *Any accident.* The stillness, the horror. Her supposedly "shattered limb" – the stillness I was becoming obsessed with, no matter that Eileen, as I heard, was *perfectly all right,* since a witness had managed to tourniquet the wound, and it was "only the leg", as Max had also said as he rushed to reassure me over the phone – she will definitely, surely, live). Which is to say, and to cut to the chase: all that preparatory steeling for the Song Dong treatment of the house only came to a halt when, after all that had happened, I decided to give up, once and for all, on *the Song Dong solution,* and take the one bit of useful advice you had urged on me from the beginning, which was to call a skip hiring company and then follow it through by emailing Lord with a sudden and probably peremptory "revision" of all we had planned. But then, almost as soon as the email was sent, how confounded I was – so utterly shocked – that I had succeeded in doing what had seemed so impossible earlier: this horrendously cruel, dismissive and heartless action. Since by giving up on my *Antipodean Song Dong solution* to the contents of the house, and calling instead for a series of skips into which I was planning to toss everything that it was possible to toss, it had started to feel to me as if I were deciding to bury the house in a gaping pit – the house and the lives of my family – to bury the five of us, and all still alive. As if my parents were stirring and awake somehow, but shaking. The five of us shaking like terrified children in the way that dad, as I imagined it, would have been shaking in his bed in the hospital, if indeed he had been as conscious in the days before he died as I've heard he was, his knees bent up like a couple of sticks that had made it into the bed along with anything else he might have been holding on to at the time – his papers, his rulers, his books, his *ideas.* And I was stunned I had done this. Distressed that I had done this – this call to order such a vast disposal. So distressed that I could do nothing but spend the whole of the afternoon and all of the next day wandering the beige linoleum floors of the shopping metropolis on the other side of the station from dad's place in Chatswood, so that I might push one of those immense Australian-style shopping trolleys around the aisles, so that I might look for and buy the various objects and fluids that struck me as useful in preparing to clear out the house. Burying myself as it were in the action of shopping and preparing – taking from the shelves of two different supermarkets and one of those *dodgy* clearance barns, bottles and bottles of cleaning products, liquids and pastes, in spray form, tubs, and those thickly S-shaped plastic vessels of noxious substances, as well as a bucket, rubber gloves (both pink and two-toned banded ones), shower caps (pink polka dots on transparent film, and the same but in grey). And rolls and packets of garbage bags: black, green, orange. In other words, *ever more objects to fill up the house,* as I could imagine you saying it. And yet the whole time I was stacking the trolleys, it had also felt as if this ordinary, everyday and very *shallow response to the house* was only possible now that I had given up on the illusion of my derivative Song Dong plans – only possible now that I was preparing to destroy my career as an artist. At least in this country. Just as I was preparing myself to fail as a daughter and a sister and a friend – even pushing myself to fail. And that I was also protecting myself from the sordid, foetid accumulation that had gathered over the decades of evasive living in our family home. That something about this depressingly cheap and mass-produced collection of plastic objects and fluorescent liquids could take the place of my supposedly "compassionate" vision, since – as I could see – it promised to be powerful and effective. It could indeed be a new, very peculiar way of making sense of it all. This idea that they, these bags of potent, fresh, new plastic objects and fluids that I had dumped on the porch – one trip after another – might offer through their cheapness and quotidian practicality, a much more immediate way of understanding the inheritance of the house, and hence play a crucial role in the making of something that could now become the "Still Lives" Wall.

II

Item: rubber gloves (medium)
Item: yellow sponges with green scrubbing side x 3
Item: garbage bags (extra-large, packet of 10) x 5
Item: vinegar (white), 2 litres
Item: Handy Andy x 2

But first, before I get to the Wall and my new approach to it – my new ideas – I should note that it struck me, as soon as I had relieved them of their crackling plastic and left them – draped them (pink rubber drapes) – over the edge of the bucket (new blue bucket with creamed-in whirls, pink rubber gloves with the fingers still sticking together, lewdly thick) – how so very *wrong* these objects looked in the house. And so you've got to imagine how it was then, with only half an hour or so before the skip was due to arrive – this unrealistic image of the gloves as they balanced rather than hung over the edge of an over-light bucket (the gloves should be hanging more loosely, I thought, they should have their own weight, rather than being so stiff, so unlikely – they should weigh the bucket down). It was their resistant, awkward approximation of the kinds of rubber gloves and buckets that you might imagine seeing in use somewhere – *in normal use* – which got me thinking that there must, already, have been buckets and gloves, surely, somewhere in the house – ones that were "perfectly fine", as mum would have said. And that *even Angus* would have had some idea of where they were. I could have rung him to ask, but also, I couldn't bear to look, couldn't bear to ring. Meaning that it was only then, when it was far too late to do anything more about getting a stronger, and perhaps more familiar-looking, bucket to start on this cleaning process – since the skip was about to arrive – that I realised how laughable was this latest attempt to subdue the house – that the most I could do, given that I wanted to do *something at least* with the things I had bought, was to see if I could push past the lengths of rescued timber and the vertical piles of *Readers Digest*s in the entrance to the kitchen to get to the sink. And only then, in the dim of the kitchen, while looking over this naff collection of cleaning objects once again – these *cleaning tools* – I could see that I was *doing it yet again* – always trying to fix things. Always trying to make things right again. Or else to *avoid*, I was thinking as I remembered what had happened with Son and Eileen, and of course, Max and Lulu. Always steering around things or else trying to make things right, and yet getting it all so wrong nonetheless. Thinking that I could well be prone, still, to the very problem I thought I had recovered from when I stopped using food and the feel of my body to gauge how things were in the world, and then to fix these world-and-me things by the very same means (that is, with my body, with food). Prone still to finding intolerable the least sorts of misunderstandings between me and others, the least confusion. Prone, too, to believing that *she* is the mad one and me (and Eileen) the sane – that *she* is the one who can never resist taking sides in a stoush or continually taking things personally (*far too personally*). Yes, prone to believing that *she* is the disordered one. The *eating disordered* one. And me (and Eileen) not anymore. And so, no matter that I have said from the beginning that I would have nothing more to say to Sonya Hervre, it being clear what she thought of me and my work after my supposedly "puke-worthy contribution" to the annual art show at Thinkspate and her consequent quote-unquote *splattered body intervention* at Nathaniel Lord's Artfest lecture the following week at the Wharf – when she dragged me into the embarrassing feud she's been carrying on with our one-time art school mentor ever since he had supposedly "written her off", as she likes to think of it, "years ago" – tagging me into her posts about the preparations for this supposed intervention all over Facebook. "Look what Thinkspate's latest show has made me think", she posted and still the comments keep coming in now and again, one after the other – the number of *shares* – that GoPro video of her disgusting preparations in her brother's flat in the Cross – the smearing of her sad, puffy and emaciated body with a rotten food concoction – "Fighting sick with sick", as she wrote in her posts. "Rotten with rotten". "Voilà 'Still Lives'" (one hundred and fifty-seven "likes", as we could count them then, of emoji manifestations: thumbs, hearts, shocked open mouths, simmering red frowns, *flowers*). No matter that I have already voiced my own opinion on Sonya's bizarre reaction to you, Teun, over Skype and even to that woman with the pastel green, blue and purplish-pink hair at Nathaniel Lord's lecture at the Wharf on the very same night – ranting, as I'm always doing, about this newfound *fluxus illness*, this wheedling two-buck trickster from the past. And so no matter that I have kept on saying that the whole of this peculiar aftermath to his annual show should stay buried and forgotten under the roll and trivia that is always coming forwards in our Facebook feeds, it could well be true that in five years time people are going to be remembering Sonya's *courageous take* on my "Still Lives" series and even on Thinkspate 2018, as Nathaniel Lord's assistant even had the hide to tell me when she rang to say that he wasn't up to our meeting the following week – this meeting where I was going to be pulling the pieces from his touring schedule anyway. No matter that I've said all this about Sonya, you have to understand how it is with me, now that I see it – this drive to get things straight, I was thinking as I stood with the bucket wedged into the sink in the kitchen and the old pipes roaring as I waited for the water to warm just a little, for any sign at all that the hot water tank was still switched on. And so thinking of course: whatever you make of my *other* reasons – my inner reasons, if you will – my decision, these last few days, to opt out of my supposedly "extraordinary vision" – this *suburban Antipodean Song Dong–inspired vision of a Chatswood house* that Nathaniel Lord and I had been planning for 2020 – to chuck it in as it's said in Oz so well – my decision has nothing to do with being outshone, as it were, by the gleam, the glutinous spit of Sonya's disgusting intervention, which even, as Eileen has got me to see, has its sane and justifiable threads. When is a person not utterly justifiable? Completely in the right? The steaming, rust-flecked chemical froth. The bucket of *greenly* poisonous water. The inevitable swaying and sloshing to get it back to the hall. The painful weight of remembering what had happened with my supposed friends digging down hard, as it seemed, into the flesh of the gloves and so into my fingers – and then, near the door, into the flattened fibres of something that had once been a soft and white-felted rug with deer and rabbits and doves and sprays of grasses on it – which is to say, into the disgusting remnant of grey-ish rag, with its crusted shadows and snags of thread that might, instead, have been nothing more than a matting of hairs. And so now, standing in such a way that I might be poised to do something about the most obvious of the sickening remnants of bacterial fluids or solids on the wall near the door in the hallway, and the fall-out from the bundle of fabric that might have been a curtain. Might have been a bedspread. Yes, standing in that familiar spot by the front door where, as a child, I used to watch the waver-ing lines and shapes in the long strip window of rippling fifties glass when mum was at the hospital with *her*, Leah. Always the long days at the hospi-tal with the one that I haven't yet had the guts to talk to you properly about. This window, then, which has always been a signally important part of the house, at least for me. Standing, watching how the world could move along its mysterious folds. This window to which I owe, as I have said in many of my artist's statements, "my whole perspective on light and distortion", my oft-quoted "interest in transparencies and solidities". This staring at the glass and the shapes that were messing themselves into the fluid of vertical striations of vinegar light. Nothing but the calm, the frantic calm of a piece of glass that wavers as it modulates everything and anything at all, which only makes it necessary to say to you, Teun, what I know will puzzle you after everything you have said about keeping clear of the both of them: of Sonya and Eileen. How I could well be depressing you with the news of what you will probably not want to hear, and which I can only bear to tell you face to face when I can talk to you properly without the phone or video-calling apps between us – without the irritating intermediary of the screen as well (where I see how your eyes are always sliding to the side, and downwards too – an infuriating preoccupation, as it always appears to me, and no doubt *my own* infuriating preoccupation as well). This need I have to tell you at last, and in definite person to person, but first in this docu-ment here – since it is always so difficult for me to say out loud any part of this – so hard to be any more direct when it comes to the *real encounter*

– telling you here, then, that something buckled in me when I went to Katoomba, and that it happened right when I saw the walking, skulking death – the *obvious anorexia* – of Eileen's youngest daughter, Lulu, as she slipped into their kitchen that Thursday morning. Yes, the way she slipped without noise or any liveliness at all into that *hippy-dippy* kitchen that was completely over-stuffed with everything imaginable – all the astonishing filth and clutter of their lives, those bits of furniture and appliances that, as I guessed, they had inherited from Eileen's mother or some other pile of unwanted remnants – say, a kerbside in the rain. The aluminium flour and sugar tins, the chipped brown enamel saucepans with their seventies-style child-patterned flowers – those saucepans that, clearly, had nowhere to live, as it were, in this chaotic kitchen. Saucepans on the floor, on the benches, on the piles of papers and oddments on the unusable sideboard – completely unsorted. And so something buckling in me right at the moment when the long, desiccated focus of this girl Lulu slipped into the kitchen past me as if I hadn't also been in the room with her – or as if I were nothing but a new excrescence on the chair she was having to avoid. And so my earlier view of what had happened to me (and also to Eileen and Sonya) in the nineteen-eighties, as it related to the confusion of our confusion with food and living – our confusion with eating – with ourselves as bodies, but mostly with our *selves* – all this suddenly becoming alien to me. Completely alien. Yes, this idea I used to have that our *issues* as we might have called them once had simply *faded* – its being just *everything else* in our lives – the objects and events and inevitably annoying people, of course – that could still get out of hand in our existence – not our selves getting out of hand, and not our bodies anymore, either – this particular view that I'd had of all this now becoming alien to me. Because how sickening it was to recall how convinced I'd been that Eileen and I, at least, had "simply got over ourselves", as I remembered saying once to her (unless it was Eileen saying it, Eileen observing it) – this notion that we'd supposedly made ourselves strong enough to resist the "restrictive images of being a woman" in the way that society dishes it up to us. That we "knew what was what" about the media, and so about ourselves as well. Yes, right from the minute I saw Lulu in the kitchen, I could see that something wasn't right in any way at all in what we had thought about this, our supposed recovery. Our *complete recovery*. And hence in everything I had said to Eileen, or she to me, about our *similar experiences* that were still too difficult to talk about, even and *especially* with each other – and also in those discussions we'd had about how to raise children differently from the way we were raised. Yes, so differently. That essential word "differently". Also, the way that, even childless – or perhaps *because* childless – I've had such a clear overview of so many families. So many children. And hence I've developed so many nuanced and ever-changing theories about how to raise children "in a far better way". But of course, I have never dared to say what I think, since *what the right?* Not to Eileen. And yet, all the same, until this moment in the kitchen with Lulu, I would have said that things had been going "surprisingly right" for her. Haven't I said this many, many times? How lovely her children. All of them lovely. And this sense that I *knew these kids so well*, even in spite of the distance. Our infrequent meet-ups. How I could *get* her children immediately, as they say it over here in Oz. This sense I used to have that, if *we'd* had kids, I would hope that our kids would have been a lot like these young women, as I have described them to you, because, yes, how clever they were – and how brilliant too. How kind, how eccentric, how "so way out", and yet *nothing like her*. These three young females, with none of that vagueness or even any of those traces of a "mincing girlishness" or obsession with appearances that we knew was so *bad*. And so *how* had they done this? Max and Eileen? None of these girls with anything but a sense of her own fierce right to exist in the world – the *goodness* of being girls as they were, and hence women-in-the-making. And also unlike so many of the girls we saw on the news – the ones that got crushed, got used, got stabbed, got flung, got lured, got killed. And hence this sickening realisation, in seeing the girl Lulu – in the state she was in – that what Eileen and I have discussed over the years about doing things *differently*, and so thought and stated and argued and observed and concluded about doing things *differently* – that nothing of what we've said, none of our ideas, was anything now but a memory of words. A memory of nothing. And so although I know that I've been *way out of line* in thinking what I've been thinking about Eileen, given what she has copped – with the accident on top of it all – *totally out of line* – I've also known that I need to tell you here that I was shocked to see Lulu. Scared to see Lulu. Even furious, I could feel it, with this old art school friend, this Eileen, this *hapless Eileen*, as she had seemed to be suddenly, at least to me – this hapless friend who had gone and run off from her family, from her kids, at the very worst moment. *Dropping her bundle*, as they say it over here. Furious with Eileen, furious with Max – furious with the astounding nothingness of a conversation that she and I had had in Newtown when we had met up only two days earlier. Because this had happened despite or even *because of* everything we had said, variously, over the years about "knowing" how to live in the world "in a far better way" – and especially how to "avoid the worst of our culture" – and so even – *even* with our very different takes on what we have generally called the patriarchal plot of the thing (subtext: anorexia) – the obsession with perfection of the thing (subtext: anorexia) – the inhibited body aspect of the thing (subtext: anorexia). Despite the way that we *at least*, if nobody else, knew how to "resist the hegemony of idealised body images", as we liked to think we had "proved" in that Bodies and Food installation at the end of art school, or so I remember saying to Eileen some years ago. And so all of this happening to us, so to speak, and despite the fact that, even with our various takes on it – our myriad discomforts, too, with trying to avoid what we didn't want to say too explicitly – we had definitely shown to the world what it meant to "resist the pressures of society" in the way it "needed to be done". That is: with the strength of our gall. Our sheer determination. Our willingness to appear crude, inexperienced, and even ugly to everyone who might have seen us sitting on those child-sized chairs and "covered with crap", as Sonya has always liked to put it – and then the whole of our lives afterwards an unwavering "resistance to the problem" as we saw it. And that even Sonya was with us on this point – as either Eileen or I have acknowledged at one time or another. Even and *especially* Sonya Hervre.

To cut forwards a little: when I set off in that rusty old car to Sonya's house in Mudgee from Eileen and Max's place in the mountains, I was keen to get it over and done with. I can even say that I felt glad – actually glad – to be doing what I was doing. Heroic even. This direct confrontation with Sonya, as I'd described it to Max during the course of making my way, as naturally and as easily as I could, down the bare, scuffed wood of their stairs to the street – those assurances I kept on giving him when he'd asked me over and over if I was okay "going out there on my own" like this, to "check out" Sonya's place to see if Eileen was there. Yes, I was driving out to Mudgee to see Sonya. To ask Sonya about Eileen. Which of course – as you can imagine – was the very last thing I'd intended to do when I heard that Eileen had left him – so suddenly leaving and not answering her phone – when, after his message to me, he had rung me on mine to ask *point blank* about "what had happened" that Tuesday with Eileen and "what the hell" I had said to her to get her so mad. Because, even though heading out west and north-west to Sonya's place was the very last thing I would ever have wanted to do, I was seeing things differently after Lulu and what I'd said about Lulu, at least to Max. So entirely differently. Because now it was *me* that had offered to drive out to Mudgee to talk to Sonya at her out-of-town property. This Sonya who wasn't answering her phone either, apparently. Yes, *me* – not that neighbour who'd come with the flowers and the cloth-wrapped homemade bread. Not any of Eileen's closest colleagues at work, or any of her "very best friends". None of them. *I* was the one that had offered to go.

To confess: by now, I was keen to do it. Impatient to do it. *This* is how to do it, I had even said out loud as I eased off the handbrake and let Max's manual-drive, nineteen-ninety-something *Aussie-style Toyota Corolla*, as I was already readying myself to describe it to you and our friends in London – this felafel-coloured car with its crusted corners – this *unbelievable pile of junk and stink* – roll forwards through the mist that was churning over the trees from the shadowy south-west end of the mountains town of Katoomba, like those great and ghostly waves that come at you in films. *This* is the way to confront your demons. I was feeling so high, so very righteous, so valiant as well. I was driving out to see them. To see them both. On my way out west to see Sonya in what she has called (on Facebook) her "seventies wino mansion" in Mudgee, where Eileen had probably gone to lay low. To demand that Sonya at least might answer my questions – and *after all this shit*, as I was even thinking in such an Oz sort of way after hearing, in Max and Eileen's house, those neighbours and colleagues carrying on and on with their theories about what had been happening with Eileen at work – the "shit at work", as one of them had been saying. "All the shit". And yet I could tell, even then, that it was going to be impossible to know – as it is still impossible to know – whether by precipitating yet another crisis with Son, I'd have been able to make any difference whatsoever to these old endemic problems – to these problems with my friends. Let alone to what I had seen when Eileen and Max's youngest daughter, Lulu, had come in on the discussion Max and I had been having that morning after I arrived in Katoomba – when she entered the kitchen where we were talking, so that she could bend over the sink to slurp like a tall parched bird at the water from the tap. This way that Lulu had pointedly ignored my presence – had even turned the sharp cogged wheel of her spine towards me, so that she could get the flow of the water as directly as she could into her mouth, the skin of her oversized trousers shivering with the effort and, possibly, irritation at the thought, unacknowledged, that I could be there with her watching.

You know, I couldn't help remembering as I steered Max's car so very tentatively – scarily – down that hill from their place in Katoomba – with the brakes down hard – wobbling around – terrified, in fact, that I would crash the car into the kerb or something worse – another car – a person, a child – a house – or perhaps only stall it – and so rolling it down the hill in neutral for a bit as I wrenched around with the gears and the clutch. Remembering how it had come to me there in Eileen and Max's kitchen, that all of us – the three of us – Sonya, Eileen and I – have always been talking about "ways" to *be* in the world. Ways to exist. Ways that, even if we couldn't quite express them as solutions to our ongoing problems with anorexia, were all intended to address – and so *resist* – what it was that had made us "like this in the first place". And of course, about how, according to Sonya, it had always been the problem *with others* that we had to resist – always "other people's agendas" that were threatening to destroy *our* agendas – to destroy our own capacities to work out how we were feeling about eating and living and just being ourselves. And so thinking again about the time I saw Sonya in Casino, which was not long after mum had died – when she told me how it was only then that she'd realised the importance of survival. The difficult and ongoing challenge of "sheer survival", as she had kept on calling it, no doubt because of what she had just been through with her ex. The jailing of her ex. The horrendous problem of his serial lies and thefts and assaults (on her, on others). Because it was clear that the world was "full of people" who were only out to "get you", as Sonya kept on saying to me in that clapboard house she was living in now that he "was safely put away" – people whose intentions were always "predatory". People whose kindness was the kindness of spiders. Active and predatory spiders. Spiders that lured you in with the sticky white pap of their kindness – their smiles and pleasantries that were always a "sham", as she put it. Nothing but the sham of their laced-out lies. These predatory people who even used the smiles and pleasantries against you in a deliberate and intentional way, after which everyone only laughed when they saw "how you fell for it", as she had realised when he was "inside" and people were looking at her "differently". It being so very difficult to deal with this situation where people seemed to think that it was *you* who was the strange one. *You* the problem. *You* who must really have "caused it all". There being no way at all that you could get them to understand that people like her ex were good at getting this to happen – where *you* would be the one to look like the bad one, the sticky one. The spider rather than the fly. Because of the way that "people like that" were always *projecting* the horror of their spidery intentions onto you until everyone believed that they were *your* intentions and not at all theirs. Everyone misreading the reality of those intentions until it finally "comes out in the wash". And then most incongruently: "when it hits the fan". And so the necessity of survival, but also the difficulty of doing so, as Sonya had wanted to tell me when I had managed to get up to Casino to stay with her – when, after not having seen her for a number of years, she had tried to describe for me how the last few months had been for her, especially. So many of us are survivors, she had then gone on to say, because we *have* to be survivors. The three of us survivors. And hence this thought that she, Eileen and I had miraculously "survived" somehow – survived the immense difficulty of the struggle to survive. The three of us managing to fight our way past those problems we'd had with "just being ourselves" in our straight-laced, prejudiced, persecutory, middle-class families, as she described them – this "struggle" we'd had when we were young and in art school and everyone was "pulling us around" all the time. Getting us to do this, and then to do that. Just as now, when she was having to push past the lies and confusion she'd been served by her ex – that netting of lies. And so the three of us, as she was saying then, having this challenge but also having been primed by our families to fight it – fighters for our own small selves in a "shitty world". Survival as a default mode of getting by, since the only way to manage it all was to keep it *out* and "be on your guard". And yet there was this sense, too, I was thinking as I was driving away from Max and his family's place in Katoomba, that the differences between us could also be important to her – vitally important. The way that Sonya had turned on me, suddenly, and in a matter of hours. How it was, then, that *I* became the powerful one, *I* the predatory one. This sudden image of myself as monstrous to a horrifying degree. How my view of the world had been flipped so easily the other way around so that, all those years when I thought I was "normal", whatever that was, it was possible that I was also, or instead, terrifyingly and dangerously wrong. Yes, my wariness of Sonya after that. The confusion of everything that had happened since Casino. Everything that culminated in Sonya's "intervention" at Nathaniel Lord's event at the Wharf. The webbing of those "nefarious" times, as even she, Sonya, might have put it. And so: me, the spider, I was thinking, while I was driving that rusty car through the backstreets of Katoomba away from Eileen and Max's place, just to get the hang of the thing. Me, the spider if I wasn't the fly. Because of course, when I had seen that young girl's emaciated body, I was once more faced with the intolerable situation of having to see *it* before me: *it*, the resistance. *It*, the anorexia. *It* in the girl. Just as if *I* were the spider that she, the girl, needed to protect herself from. Me and the world. And so the whirl of my thoughts. A sense that there was something that needed to be done or said, immediately, to help her – to resist what was happening (to *resist* her resistance), if I wasn't to be the spider to her, numbing her away. That, given all those years that I had spent in thinking about anorexia and making art about anorexia, and so *knowing anorexia*, as I thought I did, I should really have had something ready to say about it all, if I wasn't to be the spider. Something that I could do or say to her – or at least to Max. That could help her practically. The sense, then, that it was up to me, since *I knew* the illness (just as, of course, Eileen – as it only occurred to me afterwards – would have *known* the illness too). This thought, in that moment in the kitchen on that Thursday morning, that it was up to me *entirely* to speak and to act and so *save the girl*. And hence it was that I'd become seized unaccountably in the kitchen after Lulu had left – seized with the urge to proffer to Max, who was sitting there with me, something that might present itself as the *opposite* of resistance. The *opposite of anorexia*. And so how I'd become anxious to proffer what seemed, in that moment, to be the universal balm of the very thing that I was trying to enact for myself – in fact, struggling to enact in my very own life. That is, what I can only now describe as the *total solution*, as it seemed to me suddenly in Max and Eileen's kitchen, of Song Dong's method. *Song Dong's moral and aesthetic approach*, as it came to me then. And so, yes, his approach – his very careful "approach" to dealing with objects one at a time and in an orderly way, which seemed just then to be a most ingenious means of untangling what had long been tangled – a highly practical and positive means of *undoing the web* (as I saw it) that had trapped a fly. And so this urge to speak. To lean forwards and speak to Max, after Lulu had left the kitchen. To say that he might have heard from Eileen that my dad had just died and that I was now being faced with a "terrible situation" in the state of the house – a house that was "literally crammed" with "memories and stuff" – "unbelievable amounts" of stuff. *So much to do.* And about how "horrified" I had been in London when I had "thought about it all". But also how it was that I had "recently discovered" the approach of a Chinese conceptual artist to the anxious collections of his own mother, and that it was "extraordinarily useful" in helping me to see it all in "a very different way". And so how calming and methodical it was – how I could *only now* understand what it was that I needed to understand. Only now, that is, that I was "sorting it all out at last". No attempt, of course, to connect what I was saying about Chatswood and my family with Lulu. Because although I knew that Max would have known, in those seconds and minutes after Lulu had left the kitchen – when the two of us were still sitting there in silence – that I was probably thinking about her and her anorexia – because although I had known he would have realised this, I also knew that it was best not to say anything that might distress him. Nothing at all about the anorexia. Definitely *no* bald-faced allusion to the horror and fearful condition of anorexia. My sense that, surely, he (Max) would have known that I saw and hence understood that his daughter was anorexic – that I definitely *knew* – but also that he would have been glad for me *not* to talk about it directly and so to talk, instead, about *something else.* That even, and in fact, he might have been particularly glad to be supported in this possible wish: both shielded from the pain of what was going on with his daughter *at such a time* and offered something special that might even *help the family as a whole.* And so instead of saying to him that I had noticed Lulu's anorexia and that I felt really sorry about what was happening for her, and how she must be feeling bad to be in such a state – instead of saying any of this confronting – or perhaps only bleeding obvious sort of thing – I had said that I was finding it "so helpful" right now – after dad dying "and all of that" – to be sorting through the leavings of the house in an orderly and "accepting" way. And hence this talking about the Chatswood house after seeing Lulu. Even exaggerating the problems of the house, as I imagine you might expect me to do –

exaggerating the difficulties. Exaggerating the filth. Yes, the necessity of conveying right then and there what I meant by this "Song Dong approach" so that he (Max) might see what I was trying to get at. Because in that moment in the kitchen it had seemed supremely important to *get through to* Max something about this "solution" to the problems of living with the "remnants", as I put it, of the problems of others – this approach that I had only discovered "quite recently", as I said once more, and discovered in a "serendipitous way". Yes, it seemed to me then – in the several highly compressed minutes after Lulu had left the kitchen – that I *had* to get through to Max something about "my important discovery" of this method of dealing with what had once seemed *utterly impossible* to deal with – my discovery that it was *only* in this manner that it could be done, and so *only* through this very "thoughtful" method of making an orderly artwork out of everything I could find in the house. Absolutely everything. *No judgement at all.* Nothing but "empathy and order", as I was trying to say by way of making it sound very simple and attractive – and so saying once more that it was *only* by taking this much more material and orderly approach that it was going to be possible to manage what had previously seemed utterly impossible to manage in my life. Since it had occurred to me (I said to him), that it was no longer really the things, the *stuff*, that was so difficult to deal with, but the *feelings* that the objects appeared – so strangely – to embody. The horror of the objects that appeared to have been "invested", as I was coming to understand it, with "all of the problems of our families" – this "problematic inheritance" that each of us ends up with, as I was even saying to him, with one eye – I have to admit – on all that surrounded us there in the kitchen. And so my presentation of this soothingly *systematic method* of handling the objects *as* objects (even though I was yet to do any of this handling and sorting myself, no matter that I'd already been here in Australia for weeks, even then – my collections at the time being only collections in the abstract – the plastic boxes I had bought from Officeworks for the purpose of making these collections – all those plastic boxes still stacked one inside the other behind the house, near the shed – this sense that *first*

I needed to assemble enough of these boxes – that first the boxes, and then the stuff of the house). Yes, this mode of handling the objects in such a way that the feelings could be "acknowledged" for what they were, or so I was trying to convey to Max while we were still sitting at the table in the kitchen, with our dark brewed cups of tea that he had poured for us when I'd come in from their closed-in veranda that morning – this tea that was already tepid. Practically cold. These "terrible feelings" that we were all of us trying to avoid, I was saying. The disgust of the objects that is really, I said, the disgusting aspects of the "awkward people we've had to live with".

How quickly I had then stepped in behind Max when he got up suddenly towards the end of what I was saying about this "careful approach" and the disgust and the objects. I could tell something had gone wrong with what I had said. That, as usual, I had mixed it all up – saying the wrong things first. Forgoing all connection between one thing and another. And so then thinking, in my panic, that what I'd just said to him couldn't have made any sense – that I must have even sounded aggressive to him. Aggressive and desperate. But also – and despite these anxious thoughts – it also seemed to me, too, that he (Max) was *yet to be convinced* by what I was saying about the Song Dong approach to dealing with the "shit of the past", as I'd also started calling it more directly. And so thinking that if *only* I could describe it properly and in detail, and a tad less aggressively – and with a few more Oz expressions – he would be able to see how it was. That he had to under-stand it was an important – even vital – way of re-visioning the parts of our lives that we all so deeply feared. Because *he had* to realise it. In fact, as it seemed so clear to me at the time, his daughter was a *walking exam-ple* of what it meant for us not to be able to face all this (a thought that I thought but – luckily – stopped myself from putting into words). My saying how we were all so "easily swamped" by the stuff of others that we needed, rather, to categorise and sort in a systematic and open and "accepting" way. And so that *his daughter's very survival* depended on his being able to do it – this sense I had, in that moment, then, that the only way he could stop his daughter from dying as she was intent on doing was for him, Max (and Eileen, too, obviously) to make a very great effort with the stuff that surrounded them there in their house – all this stuff that they clearly had brought with them from Eileen's mother's place. Either from there or from collections on the street. And that he should act as *I* was only now beginning to act (as it seemed to me then). That he should completely re-vision the whole of his life – his and Eileen's lives – by "taking the lead" in sorting out the objects that variously mattered to him (in that "Marie Kondo way of sparking joy", as I'd said) and those that mattered to each of the others in the family. And that if he could *only* see the world as I was *only now* getting to see it – that is, through this "very simple aesthetic methodology" – all of their problems would sort themselves out and go away.

Yes, how quickly I had stepped in behind Max as he got up from the table where we had been sitting – my rush to help in any way that I could. Stepping in as closely behind him as I could manage it when he took that plastic ice-cream carton of compost from the bench beside the sink – anxious as I was not to let him get away before I could turn what I had been saying about this Song Dong approach right around. Walking out as closely as I could behind him into their garden so that I might try to lighten the tone of what I'd just been saying to him – so that I might also justify what I had said but this time in broader terms, so that it might no longer be what it must have been in fact: an assault on Max, an assault on Lulu and hence on Eileen. As if by following behind him like this – with my desperate eagerness to help – with my far too earnest effusion of eagerness and willingness (as it felt to me even at the time) – I might have been able to smooth out everything that was overly jagged in what I'd just said. And so the pathetically hopeful way I had held out the torn excuse for a flyscreen door for him so that he wouldn't have to hold it separately *with his other hand* – holding the door so it wouldn't bang shut – and then making what must have sounded to him to be several completely uncalled-for compliments about the "lush" and "verdant" state of their garden, when it was clearly a garden that had got out of hand. The depressing chaos of their garden. Yes, my forced attempt to bring together my compliments about their garden

– its "scale", its "fertility" – the flowers, too. How lovely it was looking with "those little white flower-stars" (he told me they were privet). The humming – *were they bees*, I was asking, *all over that bush at the back* (cotoneaster, he said, is a weed). How secluded, how serene it all was, I had then said, by way of trying to give something back to him all the same, since in that moment, the crisis of Eileen's leaving had to be forgotten – all of it forgotten. I just had to be *nice* again. My sole aim in that moment: to bring him round somehow, so that he could see that what I had said to him in the kitchen (and perhaps just now in the garden too) wasn't so completely out of hand. And so thinking about this painful sequence of things once more as I drove down the hill in their car towards the cliffs of Katoomba – to the outermost edges of the town where they lived – through the backstreets, so that I might become "a little more confident with driving it", as I had said to Max I would do, and of course thinking about it all yet again when I was working to wipe down the door at dad's place with one of those stiff yellow sponges that weren't so good at getting into the crevices of the flut-ings in the door frame – where god knows what had been lodging (perhaps some petrified residue of those dates that dad used to eat by the handful – always handfuls of dates and prunes to get him "going" in the mornings). Persevering with the door just as I had persevered with the driving at the beginning there, after leaving Max and Eileen's place in Katoomba, when I was still on my way to Sonya's place – the rubbery frustration of the gloves. Persevering with Max as well. And then, too, what I did and said in the after-math of being in their garden – which was clearly *too much* – outlandishly too much. My attempts (which failed) to hold up the lid of the compost bin for long enough so that Max could empty into its gaping hole – and with both of his hands – the clogs of tea leaves, vegetable peelings, brown onion shells, and the long pointed shards of burnt-edged toast – doing all of this so assiduously, *so very, very kindly* (how my hands were shaking as I fumbled with the lid). As if I could hope to modify the harshness of what I had just delivered in my appalling diatribe – in what must have sounded to him like a completely uncalled-for rant about houses and clutter and fathers and the supposedly miraculous solution of a Chinese conceptual artist who had, in fact, if I thought about it in any detail at all, made his work in a *very* different manner and a *very* different context from what I had been trying to describe for Max. And then – worst of all – that attempt to turn the conversation around towards Max himself by asking him, there in his garden – and apropos of nothing – about his *own* experiences as a teenager. Did he even come from New South Wales? I had asked so very suddenly – so very artificially. Since not only did I not know a thing about Max or his origins, as I was only then realising, but I also didn't care the least bit about what had happened to him back then. This painful silence that I myself had *gouged* into the morning, as it were, and into which I was soon compelled to pour my apparently "generous offer" to drive out to Sonya's place, west of the mountains – a long way north and west of the mountains, as he had tried to point out to me. To find out "from the horse herself", which was the expression used by one of his friends to describe this overly feared and well-known person the previous evening – to find out from Sonya where on earth Eileen had got to when she left after a fight with Max the night before.

Okay, Teun. So now you see it. This was how it happened. This was how I had offered to drive out in their car – their *other* car – to look for Eileen. But you know, in that short half-hour or so while I was working to clean the door at dad's place before the skip arrived, I got to thinking about how it was ever going to be possible to admit to anything of what I had done or said to you *in person* – any of what I had only, until this moment, managed to convey in the simplest, and hence most distorted, of ways to you in my messages or calls – as for example in Katoomba, when I Skyped you from the café near the top of the hill, near the station. When I started to tell you about how terrible it was – about how uncomfortable I was feeling in their house (the little that Max had said, and what I had tried to say as well) – when all that I said to you over Skype only got you rising fast in my defence: What kind of prick treats a person like that, you had asked with considerable anger. To think that I had *dropped everything* to help them out. Because it wasn't as if I *didn't* have a deadline, you had then said in highly sarcastic tones. Did Max know that I had a deadline? Had I thought to tell him exactly *when* I was due to be flying back to my "important work on the other side of the world"?

It wasn't so much that I lied to you then, Teun, I was thinking as I used a drenched piece of old and raggy towel that I found in the kitchen to supplement the sponge – this over-stiff sponge – so that I might get right into the crusted mechanism of the brown metal doorhandle at dad's place – wiping first with my rubber-gloved finger and then pressing in hard with the tip, even though it seemed to shift nothing of the stiffened dark bubbles in the joining parts that I'd tried to dislodge before – brown and dark from all the decades of date-smeared fingers answering the door, no doubt. Wiping, turning, and then pulling the handle so that the door swung inwards some more, back and forth, and I could see – and so test – that the handle might turn more easily in its plain metal bed – as if nothing was wrong with the door, or even the house, apart from this substance that still could not be removed entirely. It wasn't so much that I deliberately tried to distort what had happened between me and Max over Lulu (and Eileen), or indeed anything of what I hadn't meant to keep hidden from you all these years. It was just that I hadn't got round to telling you everything that had happened, or at least in the right sort of order – in the right sort of detail – which is to say in the detail and order that it needs to have, for me, but which has never actually worked as a means of telling you anything important, as we both know of course. Because when something happens, either in or with me, and I tell you about it, my telling goes awry. I start to speak to you about this thing that I want or need to speak to you about – and so doing this exactly in the way that it always appears (to me) that it *needs* to be said – and soon it starts to become *not* the thing I thought I was telling you. Not at all the thing (I thought) I was telling you. Yes, as I would quickly realise, even then as I was speaking – in the very process, the middle, the act of speaking – and even or especially when the thing that was important (to me) to describe – that I *had* to tell you – when this thing could not be received by you. When I would realise that you, in that moment, were *unable* to hear what I was trying to tell you – either that, or *I* would be unable to say what it was to you anymore. The telling about the thing in that moment failing me. The thing itself failing me. And it generally happens in the *course* of speaking the thing that I want to say, I know, or so I was thinking while I was working with the piece of old towel at the muck that was still jammed in the cracks of that doorhandle mechanism at dad's old place. It so happens that I start to say something (to you) and the something I say – or at least *think* I say – becomes something *other* so confusingly quickly that I'm scrambling to hold on to this thing that I neither recognise as mine nor know that I don't, because you and I, in the course of this speaking and listening (or at least attempts to speak or to listen), have become so anxious and stressed by what has happened that we can no longer think or listen or speak. And so it was while I was still fiddling with the towel as well as the sponge at the handle of the door while waiting for the skip to arrive out the front of the place that it became clear to me that I would need to interrupt what I wanted to say to you – and to do this even here – if I wanted you to be able to listen to this properly. That I would need to change around the order of what I was going to present to you – which is to say the ordinary and obvious order of *what actually transpired*, as people like to say over here – that is, all my thoughts and actions and realisations as they came in on me *in real time*. Yes, it became clear to me at the very front door of this place where I spent the entirety of my childhood and early adulthood that some parts of my description of what had been happening for me would have to wait, because I could see that you might need to know something *else* first. That, in fact, you might not even *be able* to keep on reading all this unless you read and thus understood this other thing first. And so I started to think about how I should actually be moving you quite a bit further on in my journey so that I could tell you here, right out – just to make things plain and clear – that once I was heading properly west in Max and Eileen's old rusty car along the Great Western Highway towards Mudgee – that is, once I had already finished with the driving practice around the streets of Katoomba that I still need to describe in more detail to you (picture me, then, as driving now along the ridge of the mountains from one town to the other in the full flow of the ordinary, regular, highway traffic) – once I was doing this properly goal-driven sort of driving, I was happy to be doing it: happy, cheered, even excited that I was doing it. This capacity I had just then – this feeling of having something significant growing in me, and growing to fruition. Becoming tight and full and rich in me. This new resolve to pin down Sonya, to get her to spill on Eileen and where she might be – to sort out this terrible misunderstanding between us all. *The heroic friend.* And so the whole time following the ridgeline of the highway, and even as the road narrowed to a crawl through Medlow Bath, Blackheath, and then Mount Victoria, and the crawl to a shuffling strain behind too many cars and trucks and stickered-over caravans that were all taking it overly cautiously on their steep descent at Victoria Pass – yes, even as it pissed me off to have to hold the old car back to a creaking grind as the gaps between the trees widened all around me to the grey blue silvery valleys on this other side of the mountains from where I should have been if I'd been serious about what I was intending to do for the house – serious about the project I had already agreed to with Nathaniel Lord – even as it was pissing me off that there were always so many obstacles blocking my way – always obstacles, always *stuff* – the whole way that I was driving west, and then north and west, I was glad to be doing what I was doing. Superbly glad. I was having an adventure. I was getting to see what I've called *the land*. Yes, I want you to understand here, right now, that what I was doing by driving north and west was actually a pleasure for me. Not at all a chore or a sacrifice. Not at all a *killing of myself* for this person Eileen (and so for Max and the kids as well), as you might have thought. And so, from this, you might be able to understand how even *I* was surprised when, instead of continuing like this all the way to Sonya's place in Mudgee – that is, *driving north and west nonstop*, as I'd said to Max (it can't be hard, I'd said, I'll just keep following the road and look out for signs) – which is to say: when, instead of pressing the accelerator to the floor as the lights ahead turned orange in the lowering sheen-roofed outskirts of a town called Lithgow – a particular set of lights, where there was also a sign nearby pointing to the Town Centre – instead of using this long flash of orange to shoot myself forwards all the faster, driving all the faster through the lights and on towards Sonya in Mudgee – I found myself pulling up short with the clutch and the brake and then, as if my feet were already deciding on their own – my arms as well – I rode the gears, as I remembered my father calling this way of doing things, and then turned the wheel so that the car jerked forwards a bit into the right-hand turning lane, and thus angled forwards, so that I was primed to turn *east* off the highway and hence, *apparently* – as it must have seemed to anyone watching – back towards the mountains, as if back towards Katoomba – back to the place I had started from earlier that day. Turning east then at a set of lights that also happened to have the overly exposed carpark of a McDonald's on the corner, where a group of children had been milling on one side of a massive van-looking thing of a car, and squabbling about something or other – possibly a parent's smartphone – because when *else* might *I* have had the chance to do this, as it suddenly seemed to me then while the car was moving with the green of the right-hand turning arrow? This chance to make a *hardly noticeable diversion* to the middle of a town (this town called Lithgow) that I'd visited so many times in the past as a child – diverting myself towards the concentrated hub of this otherwise attenuated impression of shadowy things, so that I might stock up – as it seemed that I wanted to do – on the deliciously cooled and smoky scent of *a much better time*? When the gleam of coal fumes had veiled an entire childhood, billowing its nostalgic haze over what I could only now begin to understand as the quiet regularity of those yearly family visits to Dubbo, to stay with my father's uncle Reece? That trip we often made on the Bells Line of Road over the mountains, rather than the highway, and so straight down into this valley, to Lithgow, before turning north-west to that other town, that is to Dubbo? Yes, how hauntingly, hazily clear Lithgow had been then, when I was a child, I was thinking as I followed along behind a large white and blue truck, driving along slowly now by the muffled grass by the railway line –

my sense, during this small diversion to the centre of a town that I couldn't otherwise picture very well – that there was *so much* that I had actually forgotten about my life in that house in Chatswood with my parents when I was a child. A sense of the infinity of this substance of life – of living – whose traces were, still, so difficult to find. Of the moments and thoughts and impressions that had been held together in a meld in the house – in a meldy mess, in a fragmented and filthy pile in the house – as I'd had, at this particular time during my visit, an impression only, when I'd glimpsed what I could when I pushed into the place through the back door – when I'd still been determined to begin or to at least have a look at what I was going to do for Nathaniel Lord. Because despite being only too aware of the impossibility of it all – the naivety of it all – there was still this belief that I might be about to find, in this first determined foray into the house – as much as into the fold of these low-roofed hills in dreamy Lithgow – the entirety of my childhood. Or at least some remnant of those trips we had taken to that farm where dad would clamber up the shuddering frames of windmills, and where we city-living kids would spend all the hours of daylight exploring the stiff white grass with our far more experienced but reluctant, and even "removed", *country cousins* – the black pitted sheep bones we would find – the pink-fleshed gristle still sticking to them. The luxurious humming and whining of the flies at a time when death was still something we were curious to see for ourselves. And so, after pulling up in the main street of Lithgow, by one of the shops under the knife-cut shade of a crusty iron-brown awning, and getting that surge of what had felt to me to be the warmest generosity – the fond benevolence that comes from the hum of coming to a stop in a stale-smelling car – something shifted in me. Something eased. Which is to say that, even though I had said to Max – and to everyone else – that I *wasn't* going to give her any warning at all – that I had no intention of *even talking* to her if I could avoid it. That I was just going to *turn up* – to surprise the both of them, if Eileen was there. Which is to say, even though she hadn't been answering her mobile earlier to anybody at all, I decided to ring the number that Max had given me for Sonya Hervre.

And so that pointed voice. And so that run of intention, as if she had never left off saying what she'd wanted to tell me a long time earlier. Because now I *had* to "own it", apparently. Yes, this way that Sonya kept on saying that *it was as if I had deliberately erased her as I had erased my sister*. As if I had "liquid-papered" over her whole existence. And so her asking me again and again whether I knew I'd done this and kept on doing this. Because I *constantly* did this. Her saying – cutting me off, too, when I tried to respond – how I couldn't say a thing – that it had taken her *this long* to see it all, but at least she could see it now. And so was it because *she* was sick as Leah had been sick? My sister, Leah, with the disease that – fair things fair – *I* might have inherited rather than *she*? And yet the way, Sonya said, that I would be constantly making out to the two of them – both to her and Eileen – that Leah was strange. Strange and cold as I'd always said. Always telling them about Leah and *what she was like*. But really it was *hate*, Sonya was saying then to me, as harsh as she could through the hole in the base of my phone: that is, *her* (Leah) hating *me*. She (Sonya) had been able to see it, she realised, the instant she met her (Leah) that time at my twenty-first birthday at the house, not long before Leah was killed. Her small, watchful eyes (Leah's). Hating me, as Sonya put it, and *for very good reason*. God I was vague. A soul like a plastic skin. Completely unknowing. And it must have driven my sister wild. Yes, the lies I had been fabricating all those years about me: as if it had only and ever been poor little me that was at issue – poor little anorexic me. My sister so huddled, so limited, so cold – so chronically incapacitated – but I would never say a thing about her debility. Only about *her as a person*. Always passing judgement on Leah. My *peculiar sister*, as I would call the very one who was killed so suddenly the year of the flooding. Her peculiar moods. Always getting them – that is to say, her and Eileen – to side with me, as she put it, *against this girl*. Always getting them to agree with my assessments – to agree with my overly critical standards. And so did I think they wouldn't remember that I did this? She and Eileen? Did I think they would collude in such a massive forgetting? God knows, Sonya was saying to me over the phone as I sat there in the car – hammering me with it. She and Eileen had been completely "weirded out" by what it was I'd got them to do for that final assessment, but it was too hard, at the time, to know what was wrong with the thing. Because how to explain? How hyper I had been. And completely driven. But dudes like Nathaniel Lord were always getting sucked into webs like these, she was saying. Dudes like Nathaniel Lord only saw what they wanted to see.

You know, Teun, when I was looking as carefully as I could at the door and its surrounds, so that I might make this entry part of the house, at least, as clean as I could before the skip man arrived – rubbing down the woody-ridged jamb once more (an idiotic attention, I was even thinking as I was doing it, since the stink of the process was making it far, far worse – or at least far worse smelling than it could possibly have been before I'd begun on it, despite or even *because of* the sharp green stench of Handy Andy). Yes, when, after running the dank, dripping cloth across the ridges of the rippling glass as well – all of it sluiced and dripping – and then pulling the streaming clots of hairs and dust from the tops of the skirting boards and the writing desk – and then back again along the fjords of the grim beige carpet under the remnants of the rug – when after doing all this, I noticed I was tightening in on myself – trying my hardest to get a grip, to get a handle on the whole of what had been happening, the whole of this. So not only on the disgusting wetted whorls of wire-haired dust from dad's place, which really I should have just left as they were, I was thinking as I wiped – not dampened and spread, not drooling like this. Why this urge to wet down, to dissolve? I bent over again to turn the loose and raggy towel in the bucket before I stepped out of the house to empty the hot blood water into a hole in the greyish dirt near the letterbox where someone must have pulled out one of dad's dwarf azaleas – perhaps the double red one I had given him years ago. The one that I had picked out in a hurry from the entrance to Coles. And so, yes, when I was making all this effort to clean, to rub away what was difficult, if not impossible, to remove, my attention was also and equally hard in pursuit of the thoughts that I might have just

145

poured down that hole in the garden, losing them forever, because I was still trying to work out how it was that I'd said what I said when I talked to you over Skype in Katoomba before I left for Mudgee. Even *what* I had said.

You'd asked, I think, why we were Skyping in a café again. Why again somewhere public, I remembered you asking as I went back up the porch steps to the house and pushed my way past the collapsed pile of *Readers Digest*s into the kitchen to fill up the bucket with more hot water. And it was then that I said I couldn't ask about wifi. *Obviously*, I'd added. Max being *beside himself. Poor old Max.* Making much of Max and his "terrible state" because, as I'd put it to you, then, Eileen had left him suddenly and he still was "out of his tree with grief and rage" – and so telling you about Max and Eileen, and all of the thoughts that their friends and neighbours and workmates were "coming out with" when they were trying to account for what had happened to Eileen and why she might have left Max and her teenaged children like this without any warning or clue as to where she might have gone. All that about Eileen, I was remembering, as well as the "appalling situation with Lulu", as I had first described it to you. But incoherently at first (what do you mean by Lulu's *situation*? you had asked). The way I had worked so hard to make sure, as I talked, that your thoughts and attention would stay on Max and then Eileen, and especially on Lulu. On all of their terrible and pitiable states or situations, which, as I'd tried to convince you, were "intimately related" – so that your thoughts and attention would remain somehow attached to these people who had to be pitied and worried over, and so anywhere other than why it was that I had even met up with Eileen to talk about Sonya in Newtown when I had said to you that I *wouldn't* do such a thing. And so why it was that I'd felt so caught up, so drawn, into the centre of this maelstrom, right from the beginning, and as soon as I arrived in Australia.

I kept thinking about the way that I'd told you, then, about *everything that had happened,* and in all of its detail – all of its depressingness – at least as I thought of it then. My attempts to make sure that my story of what had gone on in the last several weeks in Newtown and Katoomba would become, thereby, the accepted story – as if by telling the story *this way* – in what seemed, at the time, to be the necessary version – no matter that one part of what I said wouldn't join with the other (Why are you telling me about Lulu? you had asked with what sounded like distinct impatience – hang on, you were saying: *who* left who and *when*? And what's this with the rotten food thing at the Wharf?). As if, with every word I was saying, no matter that all of them put together weren't adding up to any sort of sense, I was still succeeding in staving off any queries you might have wanted to make about the fundamentals. So it might become clear, somehow, that the *whole time I was up there in Katoomba* I had been concerned, so very concerned that, when I had seen the anorexia of Lulu – her clearly emaciated state – I had realised I *had* to do something. That I had even been *compelled* to do something, then, *to help them out*.

Of course, even so, I knew there was no way that I could admit to you – neither then, when I talked to you in Katoomba over Skype, nor later, when I got back to Chatswood after the trip out west – no way that I could tell you that there might have been more to explain. No way that I could own up to how peculiarly *thrilled* I had been, despite my initial annoyance, my initial dismay – how thrilled I had been when I had seen how it was with Eileen's daughter, no matter that the situation was dire, with Eileen now gone, disappeared, leaving her family in the way she had done that Tuesday night, and causing all hell to break loose. And with me in such an obvious, culpable position vis-à-vis Eileen, since hadn't it been *me* to be the last to see her in person? Me *the last to talk to her properly* before her *definitely uncharacteristic behaviour* that evening? *That intense phone call with Sonya before she left*? Even that furious argument with Max over something he had done, something he had said, which *wasn't how she usually* was, he had said to me, his eyes very wide and pale and fixed. Eileen never shouts and swears. Never like this. Something had got into her, *definitely*. But if I was not able to tell you any of this then, how otherwise to describe how so very *unwelcome* I had become with Max, even with his friends who didn't know me – how to do this with you without falling in, once more, to the *other* temptation? That is, into the way it has always been so easy to describe my friends to you, and to our friends over there back home – the ones in London – in such a way that Eileen and Sonya's odd reactions, as I've called them – *their very strange reactions* – have worked to remind you of everything I should have avoided like the plague, and so: Why on earth did you stay with them? our friends would say, and of course also you: I really don't understand you. *Why did you go?*

And so that was how it happened – and how it was that once I had refreshed the bucket and started on working with a new lot of chemical-scented hot water and a sluicing of the rag and the sponge on the door itself that I realised I would have to find some way of cutting through all of this – to turn these notes I had started making in Katoomba into some more extended means of letting you know something important, something that might change your view of things. Telling you that now I can actually see that what Eileen had been trying to tell me when I saw her in Newtown that Tuesday was less about the madness of Sonya, or my role in the ongoing madness of Sonya – her extraordinary madness. And even less about what I have judged, all these years, to be the always and inevitable susceptibility of Eileen to Sonya – her readiness to give in to anything that Sonya always says and wants her to do – but rather what I have worked my hardest to avoid in everything *I* have done and everything *I* have said the whole of my life with you. Which is to say that, despite all my efforts to break free from that most abject and confusing time of my existence by leaving my family, my country, my old self behind – months and years of apparent freedom about which it has always been impossible for me to remember any more than the most crass generalities or the most painful realisations – so little of the dates, the events, that I cannot reconcile this grey water flooding of my mind with my ostensible status of becoming "one of Nathaniel Lord's brags" (Sonya's words via Eileen, apparently). Which is to say that, despite what I would prefer to call my fluke events, my weightless victories with prizes and shows, I am still as submerged in the swirls of the confusions between us that I had thought I'd left behind for good when I boarded that plane on a January afternoon at the end of the eighties, drunk on the triple excitement of leaving my friends, my family, and lying about leaving. Smudged, lost, besmirched, I will say, in what Sonya, Eileen, and I had thought we'd escaped in our last year of art school – as submerged and as lost in my submergence as ever. I should also say, as well, that Sonya might even have been right in thinking, earlier, that I had made my Thinkspate works – my "Still Lives" pieces – about the three of us – Sonya, Eileen, and me. That it was a judgement about where we had all got to now, "how pathetic we'd become" (this the wording from Sonya, via Eileen), even though it had only ever been meant to be expressing my *own* very personal experience of "drifting", as I've written in various artist's statements, "between two hemispheres of existence – south and north – embodied and cerebral" – the "stasis of infinite restlessness", as I've also written somewhere else (Prague, the Meet Factory, 2012). The figure in space. The figure in object-filled space or spaces – figure lost. Lost figure. Basically, my saying to you now that Sonya's take on all of this might no longer be so very mad, no longer so skewed and out-and-out wrong. Because otherwise how to account for how it had been *me* and me alone who had gone on to do this? No one had forced it, let alone suggested it. *I* had been the one to offer to drive Max's poo-brown rust-trap hundreds of kilometres west and north to Mudgee, to find Eileen where everyone thought she would be. *To talk to her face to face.* To go where Eileen had gone, as everyone guessed, when she had left Max and the kids and gone off in their new green Subaru Forester later on the very same day I had seen her in that café in Newtown. To Sonya's place, *to Sonya's lair.*

There, I have said it, and clearly. Long may you laugh.

It will be so hard, I can see, for you to join any of this up. In fact, it was only when I was standing out the front at dad's place again, rinsing the bucket under a garden tap that was so stiff, so old, that all it could do was drool very slow refractions down the bucket's plastic sides – it was only then that I could bear to think once more about how, after I'd set off from Max and Eileen's house, I had driven first so very pedantically around those

Katoomba backstreets. Getting into practice. Sorting things out with the gears, as I'd thought to warn Max (making much of the difficulty I was going to have with driving an old car like his), although really to calm myself down, so that I wouldn't soon come to a shuddering and hopeless standstill. How difficult it was going to be to keep myself moving, I was thinking then (and in fact as it turned out to be), because all I could think of at the time, when I'd offered to do this driving out there, was the way Max had reacted to what I'd said about my own experience of living in my parents' house – my own experience of a never-described anorexia that I was so definitely and intentionally trying to point him towards. That sudden but opaque reaction of Max that had, in turn, triggered a shock in me – that had overwhelmed me with fear, with shame, and against which – if I wanted to keep on existing – I could only push, as I was pushing in that car, through the surge of thickening fog that morning – moving the car in small and staggered bursts around the maze of Katoomba streets. *Doing my very best*, as it had to appear to Max in case he was watching.

The most I had said to you, I think, was that I had arrived in Katoomba by train that day "to be there for Max" – this emphasis on the favour I had already supposedly done. But as I drove around and around through the low-hanging sheets of fog to get more of a hang of the gears before leaving the town, I couldn't help recalling the frozen fury of Max – that image of the way that his face had closed – pulled shut – and each time I saw it again inside me my heart stopped. The clear catastrophe, as it had seemed to me then, just as it had seemed at the time, that Thursday morning – which is to say, the previous day – as I'd kept on hovering around Max and the compost bin in the garden. Trying to make amends. How small and weak and particularly abject were my offers – everything I had said – everything I had humiliated myself to ask in relation to his own life as a teenager, his own parents, his own difficulties or lack of difficulties "in growing up". Really, it was still as if he, Max, were continuing to stand in harsh silhouette against the weak, unshaded light of the living room at the end of that day, when he had padded in his thick orange socks to the doorway of the closed-in veranda where I was trying to settle for the night – doing all of his moves through the house so very patiently, and quietly, too, as if he were only making this show of being patient and quiet for me – because, as if by being so quiet, so patient now, he was doing more than he ought to do to smooth what could never be smoothed, and so never excused. The way he had, without moving his head, looked down to where I was lying or at least trying to lie among my bags and all of Max and Eileen's discarded junk in that closed-in veranda – this junk that, for all my attempts to push it up to one end of the space, away from my mat, had still rumpled and clogged around me, between me and the wall. And how he had said, with a mouth locked slightly open and a face whose expression was impossible to read, that Eileen had been *riled* when she'd come back from her coffee with me that Tuesday in Newtown. He didn't know what I had said to her that day but "she had sure been riled".

Yes, in Katoomba, I think I had tried to say something that might have helped you begin to make some sense of this when I Skyped you later that day, Teun. The day of Lulu. Starting with the way that Max had messaged me over Facebook on the Wednesday morning – and then had rung – and how, after I learned that Eileen had left the very same day I saw her, I dropped what I was doing. Yes, I'd said that, exactly, and in those words: "Dropped what I was doing" – by which I meant to show you how very quickly and easily I had called an immediate halt to the terrible, painful, but still very determined, work I had been trying to do to get this Song Dong project happening, since all I could bear to look at, for the moment, were the contents of the shed at the back of the garden – this shed I'd forgotten about. The mountainous piles of paint tins, and magazines as well, even in the shed (and, so surprisingly, newspapers, too, which, alas, were so numerous, as I had said to you not long after I'd arrived in Sydney and seen the piles of them there – so very many of them, and these going back many, many years – even to the sixties, I had said – the seventies – seventy-two, seventy-three, seventy-four – and so stiffened, so brittle and filthy with dust – and so *very* numerous – to the point, I had said, of its being a plague, a horrendous plague of newspapers). Telling you, then, over Skype, that I'd "dropped" where I'd got to on this Song Dong–inspired project on my father's house – this attempt that, as I couldn't bear to tell you then – no way could I tell you – had already become stuck. And so the weeks of not being able to admit to you that it was agonizing – how even the apparently easiest categories of objects in the shed had been impossible to approach in any way at all. Since I kept finding that I was always being overwhelmed by the difficulties of determining *what* constituted the objects that needed to be gathered and those to be disposed of. Since the entirety of what was there in the shed, as I saw it, had seemed so boundless – the distinctions between what even dad might have considered to be rubbish, such as the rat droppings, the fallen flakes of paint from the walls (and yet my readiness to imagine collecting even these), and what could never be considered rubbish, even by him. What was important but just neglected. And so the whole of it, for the moment, left in place – as if concreted in – because it had been impossible for me, then, to decide what to do with it – even how to start. How one category of objects was always infecting another. And so how to decide. The intact newspapers, for instance, and the not-so-intact ones – the clearly discarded ones. The not-so-discarded. And then all of the dried and stinking clothing that I discovered the only time I'd managed to force myself into the house through the back door, with the triangle of blue-white light streaming from the end of my phone – the clothing that must have gone back, if only a few weeks, until the time that Angus had left. This need to work out whether these leavings of clothing were the kinds of objects to be collected *as is* or not – that is, arranged in some sort of relation to the collection of shirts that were still hanging neat and quiet in the cupboard, with their lines of dust on the run of their shoulders, the pots of odoriferous ointments left next to the bathroom wash basin, half of the lids undone. The scuffs of skin, of toenail clippings. The millimetre dustings of grey and white bristles in the basin and all over the floor – everywhere in fact, peppering the dramatically lit nebulae of dust that had rolled away as I moved in among it on the floor in my shoes. Forcing my way that time into the bathroom. The bedclothes in a pile in a wedge-shaped tower in the corner of it, the sheets and blankets one after another, and all of them stained somewhere, as I could see as the light moved over them, even without touching them. And then, what I should have been so pleased to see, but of course was not: that cardboard box in the middle of the bath – this box that was split at its sides with all the drawings that Leah and I had ever done as children. Each, as I imagined it, of the pictures of animals and houses (hers) and people and flowers (mine). And also, in an ancient red and white Grace Bros plastic bag that was shoved between the bath and the old wicker basket that used to hold the dirty clothes – there in that split, disintegrating bag: what must have been all of the remnant newspaper cuttings that mum had kept in the nineties and noughties for me – so many torn-out pieces of print that were labelled with my name and a date and, obviously, never ever passed on to me. And most disturbing of all: dangling from the end of a short length of dark grey cord – which itself was plugged into the broken star of a bared ceiling socket – the largest incandescent bulb I had ever seen in my life, whose collar, I could see, had been labelled with a browning section of masking tape that revealed the determinedly meticulous and definitely recognisable markings of my father's hand.

How ready I was to stop this attempt to effect the Song Dong solution to the house the very second that Max's message had come in on my phone about Eileen taking off and leaving him. So very relieved, in fact, that I was compelled to respond and thus to have this reason to leave the house. Relieved – even if I resented the intrusion – definitely resented the delay – that I could now do something decisive. That I would need to turn around where I was (which was standing, once more, in the back garden and staring into the gloom of the shed). That I would need to walk back up the hill to the Airbnb and from there to the station to take the two trains to Katoomba to help Max work out what might have happened just after I'd met up with Eileen in Newtown the day before.

Of course, in Katoomba, in that café where we Skyped, Teun, I was not yet able to tell you that when I'd dropped what I was doing at that moment to help out Max I was definitively dropping it – everything and all of it. Instead, what I said to you in digital face to face was that I'd got on the train at Chatswood as soon I could after talking to Max, and after this, the main thing you'd wanted to know was not whether I was still going to be up to continuing with my Dong-inspired project on the house, but why it was that, despite your constant reminders, your nagging and nagging, that I *keep my independence* by making use of dad's car, I'd gone and put myself in such a vulnerable position *yet again*? You didn't want me to forget, you were saying, the last time I visited *one of my Australian friends* – by which you were thinking of Sonya very obviously. Of that time I travelled to Casino by train and was stuck for over a week in that clapboard house by the river, because it had been impossible to ask her to take me back into town again in her car. Such a state she'd got into not long after I arrived, as you reminded me, that I'd dared not utter a single word. A poisonous state. Surely I hadn't forgotten it? The anger, the difficulty having been all in my head, it was true, but all the same, as you said, this certainly didn't help me sort out the problem any more easily – so stuck had I been for years now with the "nonsensical notion" that I'd offended my old friend Sonya Hervre not long after I arrived. My insisting to you that her entire demeanour towards me had changed all of a sudden, early on while I was there – it being impossible to know the cause or to probe it, as I'd said to you, at least at first, as soon as I came home to London, although I'd secretly known – and had always known. That weekend in Casino that turned out to be the longest of long weekends – a weekend that turned into a week. A torturous week. Every day having to tiptoe around the house as Sonya worked in her studio at the front of it – every day walking the forty-five minutes to the shops and the forty-five minutes back because it seemed that I needed to cook for her the whole time I was there. It being *the very least* I could do, as I'd felt at the time. And especially since it had been *me* who had lobbed myself in with her – *me* who had imposed. Because I'd known I'd just have to do this if I wanted to have any hope whatsoever of even beginning to make up for what I'd said that first night – for what had to have been an insensitive way of putting things, especially after what she'd been telling me about how difficult life had been for her recently. This sense that it was all very likely to do with what I had told her about my artist's residency in Hoorn – that residency I'd mentioned – and "boasted about" apparently. Just the fact of the residency needing to be countered in some way, it seemed, since the mentioning of Hoorn and what I had been doing there had prompted in Sonya, as I remembered it, an instant reaction. That change of mood. Although first of all, there had been the dinner in her kitchen at the back of that house in Casino, with her laughing about "everything" we had been through together in Camperdown and at art school – our "shared tendencies", as she called it. Our problems with living with the "shit of things and other people", and so with her *telling me everything*, and in the way she has always liked to emphasise things with that snippety laugh of hers, as I'd imitated for you all those years ago. The mess with her *physio man*, as she called him, who had brought her to Casino – even "lured" her to Casino. Who turned out to be a "freak", an utter crazy, "psycho arsehole". Who had, the whole time, been running from a number of criminal charges – several of them rape. The very least of them fraud. His "god-awful mates", as she had discovered the first day she arrived in the town. How he was always going driving with them – somewhere into the bush, to some place or other where there'd always be *things to collect*. The way he'd always be leaving off what they were doing together, such as when they were cooking, or shopping, or even when they were in bed, just so that he could fit in with those friends. The way, it was clear, even from the very first day – when one of them had called and he'd got up from where they were sitting out the front of a café and had walked off, leaving her there – that her *physio man* had "completely changed". But how, nonetheless – and despite all of the problems – the scare of it all – it had been a blessing of sorts, since he was now "inside", and she had escaped being implicated in the arrest. This "tacky" little house she had landed when the neighbour had stepped in to help – an unforeseen blessing, really, this crappy bit of house that still belonged to the neighbour's mother but suited her fine while she was *settling her options* now that the MS symptoms were coming back "with a vengeance" – the numbness again – the whole shitty lot of it, and probably due to the stress. And yet – would I believe it? – the number of artists up here in the town, she'd said as she leaned back in her chair and gestured with her fork at the darkness outside, at her "Casino art world", as she called it. This extraordinary place. Her "poncy family" would never believe it – that is, if she ever got round to telling them, which she knew she wouldn't (why they needed to know about anything in her life at all would never make sense to her, since they could never be happy with a single thing that she did). The luck of this "art world", as she kept on calling it. Which was how I had thought of telling her about my residency in Hoorn – this tiny place in the Netherlands, I said, by way of an offer from my part – a gesture – a continuing on of the conversation, as I saw it. Hoorn being not so much bigger than Casino, I was guessing, or at least I had said – my problem with numbers coming to the fore. The one figure in the thousands, the other in the thousands, too, but obviously nothing alike, as you had pointed out the first time I told you about what I had said to her when I was staying in Casino. What number exactly? It had been confusing to me, since I'd thought the population in Casino was more or less the same as Hoorn, as I'd said to you much later. But of course it was nothing like the same. This momentary confusion I'd had about these two small places – the one so much smaller, it seemed, than the other, but both in my mind, at the time, virtually the same. And so telling Sonya in Casino about my stay, my residency in Hoorn – in this place that, despite its size, ran a number of museums, and some of them even very well known. These tiny places, I was saying to her, being "always surprising". Its only having become obvious to me later (or so you thought to remind me in the café in Katoomba), that it hadn't been such a great idea to refer to the museums in Hoorn – that I hadn't needed to say this thing about Hoorn at all. That really I shouldn't have mentioned the residency either – this delicate topic of residencies, let alone Europe or museums or the fact of my having been chosen, I was realising even as you were talking about residencies – and chosen for anything that related to art or the art world *in any manifestation*. And so the awareness of my gaffe with Sonya arriving in a single instant, as I was remembering once more in the café in Katoomba while you were talking. The awareness arriving virtually immediately after I said the word "Hoorn", but also arriving an instant too late. And so the mood in the house by the river changing so very suddenly – how quickly, as I remembered saying to you sometime afterwards in London, did the poison settle in. Hence, in Casino: my precipitous attempt to explain away the residency in Hoorn – my precipitous attempt to defuse what, it appeared, I had created *ex nihilo*. My monstrous *faux pas*. The residency in Hoorn that I had landed, so to speak, and which had suddenly become wanton and decadent, tasteless and selfish. My description of Hoorn, and so of Casino and Hoorn, all wrong, so horrifyingly wrong. And even my explanations to Sonya about you and your family – your brother-in-law – at the museum whose connections had helped with the application – this bizarre attempt, as it seemed to me later, to try to formulate, all of a sudden, the most ordinary-sounding explanation of what otherwise, from the perspective of Casino in Australia, would have seemed such a gross demonstration of my undeserved wankery. This bizarre attempt of mine to try to make nothing of Hoorn, which, far from reassuring my Aussie friend and one-time art school class mate Sonya Hervre, seemed to inflame her envy – even her dislike – her flagrant dislike – of me all the more, as I longed to put it to you and any of our friends in the years that followed after I returned to London, but really couldn't bear to get anywhere near. All these tiny or, as you've called what little I've shared, "microscopic details" of our "famous falling out", about which you nonetheless reminded me in Katoomba and which, along with everything else that was going through my head at the time, ended up prompting the very first of these notes to you (how I started to type them up on my iPad in Katoomba library immediately after talking to you in that café up the hill). All these confusing ways that I have said one thing to you at the very same time that I have been thinking another, and which still weren't so clear to me when I was muddling along in Max's old car early on in my journey out west – still driving through the empty, misted-out streets in Katoomba early the next day – when it was best just to concentrate on the repetitions of first and then second and then third gears (and then second and first) with my left hand joining the silence of the increasing cloud. The soothing cloud, and the gaps where I could see the asphalt through it – dark through the light. And now, with the skip so soon to arrive at dad's place – as I was thinking while I was rinsing the bucket, still, under the tap – finding myself somehow doubling with it all – the doing and the thinking. How it all seems so feverish – all of this, I was thinking – everything I did then in my attempt to "help". Thinking of the great awful tangle of Sonya and Casino, and even of you – my conversations with you – as I knocked the bucket upside down on the grass and then went back inside. So that I could continue with the clearing for a while instead of trying to make any more sense of it all. I bent down to haul out a clotting of overalls and a towel that I'd found wedged behind the fence posts near the doorway to the kitchen – pulling it all along, out the door, down the stairs and leaving it in a sprawl on the pile of things by the driveway – splayed and all the more disgusting than it might have been, since it was all so foully moist. These details about Sonya and Max and even our conversation in Katoomba, too, that are, inevitably, painful to recall, I was thinking as I was also trying *not* to think, then, in Chatswood. Yes, all so painful, even though there were also those other more luminous details – such as how, as I discovered that morning in Katoomba when, after looking for somewhere I could begin to make some sense of my thoughts after talking to you over Skype – anywhere that wasn't in Max and Eileen's house – where else to go? – I found that new, immaculate library where I sat by the window, in one of those curved and cute plastic seats in primary colours that had a view onto the courtyard – a seat for a child, I'd thought, with a view of the rain, of the white of the sky – so I might *take it all in* but also very simply, too, as a child would normally do (this thought occurring to me then). A child that just starts to draw. This particular detail of realising how it was good to do something active with my pain, to type something

158

here – indeed anything at all – onto the otherwise inadequate screen of my mini iPad. And so, during the process of that early typing – and now once more as I've been remembering what it was like to begin these small unfurlings as I continue working at the same document here – in this emptied-out house – putting more and more of these details down onto this screen even if, as I can also guess, they will be *way too much* for you. Because this you had said to me that memorable time after I'd returned home after visiting Sonya at the end of that journey to Oz – way too much, as you'd said not long before I fell asleep – my face nodding into the meal you'd prepared for me – while it was still so light and airy outside. Way too much, which was how it had also been for me when you had attempted, over Skype, to remind me about Sonya's reaction to the residency in Hoorn, as well as *that week long torture in Casino*, as I know I have put it in any number of versions to you and our London friends. *Way too much*, as I should have said to you in that Katoomba café, when you tried to tell me the story yet again – when I wished you would stop – the word "Hoorn" having now become synonymous with poison. Because how to say any of this to you, I was thinking when I began to write the first of these notes that I have since expanded into this longer explanation. I should have definitely told you that I didn't want to listen to what you were saying to me anymore. This repetition of me to me. That, in fact, just by hearing the story about Casino *yet again* I was being reminded of the way that your chivalrous reactions to Sonya's reactions have always been tainted and even skewed by something that was overly familiar to me – probably because it was just a mirroring of *my* kind of thinking. Because it was also in *my* kind of words. And yet also because the words were not really mine anymore, since the *mine* had now become *yours*. And hence how it must have seemed to anyone else who might have been listening to us as we were talking to each other in that café in Katoomba – even to Sonya herself, if she'd been there, in a chair behind me, say – one of my very worst nightmares – being caught like this. So very *caught out*. This realisation that, although I didn't recognise what you were saying to me at the time – after all, it had sounded so wrong, so highly presumptuous, so totally out of whack – *I* was nonetheless responsible for it. And this was because I had also realised, then, that *I* had been the one that had concocted the tone, even the substance, of what you were saying so very warmly in my defence – in your heroic and even indignant reaction to what I had started to say about Eileen and Max, and which was now being dragged from what I had said to you many years earlier (but in London) about Hoorn and Casino. Can't my Australian friends cope with the very smallest of my successes as an artist? you were asking me, probably by way of trying to bolster my confidence, my resolve. Sonya is mad, you had said to me, then, over Skype. She's definitely mad.

And so in the house in Chatswood, remembering all this – the way that I was thinking about it obsessively then, too, as I was driving away from Max and Eileen's house the day after I Skyped you. Never telling you what I was going to do, of course – the idea of the journey to Mudgee and Sonya having arrived so suddenly and so very painfully to me. This journey that I needed to get over and done with fast, now that I had told Max that I was going to do it. Think of it as lancing a boil, I had even said to myself, in those early moments as I wended my anxious, juddering way down the slopes of Katoomba in his rusting, smelly old car without noticing a single detail of the streets that I was driving along on my way to the end of the town that would lead, eventually, out onto the Great Western Highway. Just to get into practice. Nothing but the awkward changing of gears and the attempts to ease out the clutch without stalling when I stopped at an intersection – first, in the lower streets of the town, before I turned to head back up to the ridge again, along the main street, and so out onto the high-way. Doing all this, that is, until I turned a corner into a jam of steaming cars behind a giant, fridge-coloured coach, and so stalling – the sound of the engine shuddering dead – in a spot that I might have even wanted to see again, even though I hadn't consciously looked out for it. This spot that would have been a vista from Echo Point of the so-named Three Sisters – you know, that famous outcropping of tiered, bared rocks that I have told you about before. Stalling in the car right where there might have been a glimpse, even from the road, of these fabled rocks if the spume of the valleys hadn't been pouring up and over the sides of the cliffs and drowning it all. Stalling in the car near where the tourists I could see on the plaza beside me were hurrying along with their heads tipped forwards, some with the useless frames of umbrellas as the mist kept pushing its fat white fingers through what could be seen of the leaves and the branches and, somehow, through the seals around the doors into the car as well. Pushing, too, into where I was sitting between the sides of the Corolla that still smelled – as I planned to describe it to you (as well as our friends when I got back to London) – of a loose and saggy seventies-style vinyl – a dark grey vinyl over a shrunken and oily foam. Which is to say of the moist and yellowish-brown smell of the version of Australia I had never properly left when I left at the end of the eighties, and which will always pull after me – will always stay attached to some part of my body. The leaves of the bush, I would say, but also this vinyl. The chill and the rubbery pathos. And so here being struck by the silence, too, as I watched the people hurrying and then sinking out of sight as they moved towards what had to have been the edge of the land and hence towards the edge of all that I could remember of this place that I thought I knew. Which meant that instead of being able to enjoy, as I have thought of it since, the beauty and the strangeness of what I was seeing or at least emerging through what I was seeing, my thoughts seemed to push right back into the deep ridged rut that they were running in earlier. And so it was that I started up the car again and launched myself back into the blinding white of the mist, no longer thinking about the vastness of the valley that I remembered being here, out of my sight – the extraordinary vista I had once seen for myself the last and only time I had visited Eileen and Max together. The ridges, the valleys. An impossible scale of landscape, where the smallest of the white dots I had seen circling below me had actually been birds that were the size of apes. And so not thinking about how very ancient and beautiful and complex was this land that I had only ever wondered about during my years of living in London – and so not about the cultures I had never known much about either. Nothing, absolutely nothing, I had said, when people used to ask me about what I knew of the Aboriginal peoples who had lived where I used to live – nothing but the names of a few of the suburbs. Nothing. Yes, instead of trying to get some idea of the immensity of everything that I failed to understand and now couldn't even see for myself, all I could think of as I started off driving again, so slowly through the mist – anxious about avoiding other cars – cars and people – all I could think about at this time, when I might have taken the opportunity to sit very still and think about where I was *properly* – all I was thinking about, then, Teun, was how I was going to be able to admit all this to you. That is, what it was that I was now committed to doing in relation to seeing Sonya again. This way that I was *always getting caught up* with trying to make sense of my precipitous actions – my peculiar need to make careful and rational justifications for everything I did. As if my life were comprised of nothing but one elaborate justification after another, and each of them concocted. One at a time – just to make temporary sense of what I would otherwise be unable to account for. And how it was like my earlier concern – my difficulty in telling you about being in Katoomba at all. Which is to say why it was that, despite your entirely comprehensible concern that I be ready, at a pinch – even in the middle of the night – to find my own way out so that I could get away from my friends whenever I needed to – *when and if it got too much*, as you had said to me in London, and as I was remembering once more when I got Max's old brown car pushing somehow, my heart racing, from one gear to another through the baffling white – this *completely hysterical irony*, as I planned to call it one day if I could, by way of holding myself and my intentions together as I spoke, if only to make something out of the confused position I seemed to be always finding myself in. The way I would say, or at least was resolving to say, then, as I slipped through the knots of those confounding streets in the lower backstreets of Katoomba – surprisingly narrow – surprisingly filled with cars and people – saying that, given *everything* that had happened over here with this trip, it hadn't in fact occurred to me to drive my father's old car. That, actually I'd been much more in tune with you right from the beginning about this concern of yours about that car than I had been able to admit to you over Skype in that café. That, despite what I'd said then in defence of my trip in the train, I hadn't felt up to driving dad's old Fairmont *at any time* here – never once wanting to get into that stretched and flattened blue wagon that my father had kept, miraculously, still "in rego" (as they call it here). That ship of a car that always looked as if it could sail its way to the foothills of these mountains, tacking across the haze of the suburban asphalt between Sydney and Katoomba to run aground god knows where and with a mind of its own, as I remembered describing to you and several of our London friends – perhaps even Arijit and Franz. My father's car having become, to you – to them – but only as I'd imagined it – some kind of mythical and wondrous vessel. A symbol of the Australia that I saw you all liking to tuck into your personal globes of the world. The kind of Australia that, with its garish and lovable eccentricities, its spatial extravagance, its kooky charm, must continue to exist if nothing else did. So that where they and we lived – and where they and we loved to go in London – and everywhere else in our immediately familiar sort of orbit – basically, so that all of our in fact only obscurely understood part of the world might become a lot more clear and right and rational as a result of this sketching in for you – *for you all* – of the outlandish car that had belonged to my dad. The lovable stupidity of Australia, as I told it. This car and what I would do with it. This need, as I imagined it, for this car to be kept on its shelf as a brash, eccentric object so that we, in our international – our *super*-national mega metropolis – might not mind so much that the East End we'd loved for so long was changing. That money was moving in and had moved in long, long ago – or worse – that all those people who, simply, were different from us in some way that it was difficult to describe – richer? more self-possessed? more intolerant-looking? – were shoving around on our streets. Even talking out loud about our streets in a way that made us awkward, uncomfortable. Their "Brexit mindset", as we'd been calling it – changing everything – narrowing it, too. Their *Brexit minds*. This peculiar need, I only realised as I was talking to you over Skype in the café up the hill from Max and his daughters in Katoomba, to account for why I had failed, so suddenly – and so entirely uncharacteristically as it seemed – to follow through on what had to be, from the first, my cherished dream: this whim that I had indulged in with you in London when I had said I would drive that monstrous thing if I drove in Australia anywhere at all, and especially to the mountains. *Anywhere out of the city*, I'd said. That I would wind the windows down so that my hair would fly back until it plastered my skull, calling greetings to *Ustra(l)ya* as I drove. This dream that I devised for no other reason than to whip up the thoughts of our friends and you and me to an incredible pitch – to ridiculous heights – Sonya and the car. All of them ridiculous and large. So easily laughed at. And then this way that, suddenly, all of it changed. The seriousness. The clash between what I had said to you several years earlier, and what I had said to you over Skype in Katoomba. My attempts to calm all of it down, to smother what I could. Since *the situation with Max and Eileen was completely different from the one with Son*, I'd said. My hurried explanation that here there was no rapist ex-boyfriend lingering, muttering, in a jail. No art-cluttered, old-ladyish clapboard house without curtains. No terrible moods, no faraway railway station, and – most significant of all – no darkly poisonous, or even outlandishly incomprehensible, Sonya. This picture of the situation of Eileen and Max and their daughters in Katoomba, notwithstanding how so very strange I was finding it – and troubling too – especially my own reactions to it all, which I couldn't admit to. This image of these *other friends* that I had – that I needed, then, for you to understand – these other friends needing to be a clear exception to everything I had said before. A *necessary* exception to all the stories about my friends and their crazy sorts of antics here in Australia that I have tended to tell you and our friends about these last several years.

Hence my concern to tell you over Skype in that café before I'd left to drive out west – telling you that not only was I, in Katoomba, much, much closer to the station than I was in Casino – so much closer, I'd said (I could almost walk in my sleep to the train, could follow a path that went upwards, always upwards). And not only all this, which was important and even fundamental to my experience of being here, as I had tried to tell you, with the awkwardness of someone who speaks so seriously only when she is meaning to speak in another tone entirely – Katoomba and Casino being *hardly the same* – as I'd then tried to say in a lighter tone. Not only all this about the convenience, then, because it had now become essential to convey to you over Skype, if I could manage it, the significant point that Eileen was different – that she had always been completely different from Sonya. Eileen, as I had said to you not long into our virtual conversation in Katoomba, having never had the intensity and madness of Sonya, even though all of the time I was saying this, I was plainly aware that the words "intensity" and "madness" were something of an exaggeration, or at least a distortion, after what Eileen had been trying to tell me in Newtown – these words "intensity" and "madness", which, since Casino, have long been associated with Sonya in every conversation I've had with you whenever you or I discuss Australia and my friends over here – *my Australian friends* – or describe them to any one of our friends in London, Reims or anywhere in the Netherlands. And which realisation as I was driving around in those backstreets of Katoomba – and even earlier, as I spoke to you over Skype the day before in the very same town – made me weak, so sickly weak in the pit of my stomach, because it was only then that I began to understand how often I lie without exactly knowing it at the time. Since I was remembering how important it had seemed for me to remind you over Skype – even if I didn't quite believe it then as I was speaking – that when Eileen and Sonya had lived together in Wollongong all those years ago, the intensity and madness of Sonya had been entirely on *her* side of the two of them and on her side alone, no matter that it had always, then, been Sonya complaining about Eileen – Sonya always identifying the "super crazy" set of claims, as she used to say, that Eileen would regale their visitors with if she (Sonya) let her. The way she would say that Eileen really should never have begun the studies in social work after she'd given up on art as a career. That people who did social work, and particularly psychology, were always entirely mad themselves. That in her (that is, Sonya's) experience, people who "did" psychology were only ever intent on solving their own intractable problems, and while they were inevitably drawn – in fact *sucked fully into* the intractable problems of their clients – this unfortunate side effect, which they liked to call "burn-out" (said Sonya), was nothing but an inevitable extension of their *own* hopeless predicament, their *own* gaping difficulty, with existence. And that by simply enrolling themselves into these kinds of courses, they were already declaring themselves "right up front" to be the very worst possible candidate for doing such a course or ever practising either as a social worker or a clinical psychologist. The very intensity of her argument at the time being enough to disquieten me – the madness of Eileen having never been as obvious as the madness of Sonya, as it has always seemed to me the instant I got any distance from the apparently clear and cogent conviction that would tend to infuse the words that Sonya always introduced in her own defence – any distance at all from the tangle of her otherwise very logical if elaborate spiel. And so from the peculiar webbing of Sonya's mind. As I spoke to you that time in the café at the top of the hill in Katoomba, then, about my sudden decision (although after the fact) to travel up to the mountaintop town to help out Max – and despite all my efforts thus far this trip to avoid what you have been calling "those crazy friends" (Hadn't I said that I would always remember to keep the furthest distance possible from them? Hadn't I said to you don't worry, if they call, I'll run *in the very opposite direction*?) – as I spoke to you there, while leaning over my iPad, so that it looked as if I were leaning over a long and narrow well, I found myself trying to convince both myself and you that I had never really said that my friends were as crazy as you seemed to be saying. And that it might even be the case that *you* were misjudging Eileen and her family as a result, simply, of that first very odd, or should I say highly depressing, visit I paid her after she and Max had moved up there, which happened to be associated in my mind not only with the death of my mother but also with that visit to Sonya in Casino a week or so later – which I should never have described to you in the way that I had, I realised (I said). And so as a result of that, as well as everything, very likely, that

Sonya has told me in the past about Eileen – and so anything I might have inadvertently passed on to you in my descriptions of those times – or rather, of my Australian artist friends and their lives. Because, in fact, as I said that time in the café in Katoomba the day before I set out in Max's old car to find them, it had always been Sonya that I was most cautious around, *never Eileen*. Always Sonya that I had to protect my sanity from, just as I also had to protect any and all of my artistic ideas from Sonya, too. Always Sonya who had encroached, from the beginning, on anything that was central to what I had been trying to develop all those years ago at art school. For the entire time the problem with my art, my sense of self, had always to do with Sonya, and never with Eileen, who had rather tended to stir in me a very tiring sense of obligation and occasional irritation. And if I had said any more than this about Eileen, I was saying to you over Skype in the Katoomba café, it was likely to have come simply from my mood at the time. Since every time I have returned to Sydney after my supposedly definitive exit at the end of the eighties, I have never felt relaxed or happy or glad to be home in the way that people have always wanted me to describe it, but only annoyed and hemmed in by all the obligations that I have never been able to meet. So, as I said to you then, it was never going to be a problem that I didn't end up driving a car to the mountains "to keep my independence", since it has never been at all difficult trying to leave Eileen's place when I wanted to. It has never been like that in any way at all. In fact, if Eileen had been here in her house, I said, she would probably have just been a little too over-concerned about my other obligations. Over-concerned, for example, that I might have stayed out too late or away from the problem of my father's house for too long. Her over-concern – as it would seem to me when I was with her – about this house and this father whom she had never really known but whose sudden death she had heard about, if not over Facebook, since she's not so *au fait* with Facebook, as she had told me several times during our meeting in Newtown, despite what seemed to be evidence to the contrary – if not over Facebook, then somehow "on the grapevine", as she has always put it. It often being Eileen who comes forward with the kinds of excuses and also very valid reasons for leaving – *her* reasons for *my* leaving, very oddly – that really I should be using myself if I were sufficiently in touch with my own concerns before the point where I get – as I do so often get (I was saying to you over Skype that time in Katoomba – reminding you then of other conversations we'd had in London, earlier in the year) – yes, before the point where I get to *complete desperation*. You needed to understand then, I was trying to say, that Eileen has never been someone who expects, and expects for too long or makes it difficult for others to do what they need to do, or what they want to do – or at least never been the one to push the whole slow weight of her pain-filled self on you – using this pain, this self, to wear you down, as I might have implied on other occasions and in other conversations. If anything, she is someone who tries to slip the very right words into your mouth, I'd said. The very right words but with the wrong kind of tone. Who puts the words that you know you should be using in the places in the sentence where you, not she, should be using them (and so: Thank you for reminding me of this, you might say, if you really felt thankful for her help). This way she would put the words in there and then you would get the feeling that those *necessary words* were so way off kilter that you could do nothing but reject them automatically – gag and eject them straight from your throat. There being no way that you could absorb those words and take them into yourself as you should – as anyone else would be able to do in a similar position. Absorbing and using them, as you would always think you should be able to do – as anyone else who needed to learn and who, with a recently deceased father, should really have known *herself* how to do or say, and so should have thought of doing without such prompting. And so this Eileen who makes, by her very conscientious attempts to see you, to describe you, as the person you ought to have been if you'd had any human feeling in your body – any compassion at all for the father who had fathered you – who had cared for you – and now was, *sadly, beyond all care*. This Eileen who makes you feel, by the very gap in your feelings, where such feelings should be, that you are no way even close to being the sort of person she has always thought you were – that person you might have wished to be, or at least seemed to be, but who always, inevitably, falls short in an embarrassing way. If anything, as I had said to you when I'd gone to the café up the hill in Katoomba to "touch base", as we called it after my strange encounter with Max and his daughter, and so before seeking out the quiet and relief of the library that the girl in the café had described to me, where I made a start on the notes in this document here – making notes about everything I had said and everything I had ended up doing despite what I had intended to do on this trip in terms of my career, as you put it before I left for Australia – the once-in-a-lifetime opportunity to create an *Antipodean Song Dong– style installation in suburban Sydney* – notes that I can only begin to make sense of and write out in some sort of continuous state now that I have gone so very deeply into the problem of the house and its effect on me. If anything, and contrary to everything Sonya has always said, Eileen is *exactly right* for that work she did when she started at that supposedly disadvantaged school's after-care centre as the art facilitator, coordinating the shop-side graffiti project opposite Punchbowl station with extraordinary ease, as it seemed to me when she described what she'd done for the community. The way she had seemed to know what each of the kids was thinking and feeling – all of their anger and jealousy and showing-off verve. All of the stories that Eileen had come back to us with: the "family circumstances" of one, where the mother had such addiction problems that her kids, from the eldest to the youngest, had had to hide from her the smallest of objects. The five-year-old pocketing the white rubber plug to the laundry sink for his own convincing, individual reasons. If anything, too, no matter that Eileen had annoyed me that Tuesday when we met up in Newtown, as I'd said to you earlier, Teun – driving me *totally insane*, exactly as I'd predicted – her too ready, too immediate, too earnest defence of Sonya (the whole time taking the part of Sonya) – no matter that she'd done this, as I'd said to you, I could also now admit that Eileen was also – which was maddening – exactly in the right about everything that she had been trying to tell me about Son. This Sonya who – *unlike Eileen* – will never spare a single detail of anybody's flaw, any problem, anything less than the best. My *perfectable best*, as Eileen probably thinks she is helping me to attain (on Sonya's behalf). In fact, I can only wonder, as I'd even said to you in Katoomba – I can really only wonder whether Eileen, in Newtown that Tuesday, had been trying to tell me about what was on her *own* mind, too: in other words, about her own desperation. Her readiness to leave everything behind her – to slide a wedge into a crack that might already have been running all the way down and through the centre of herself. That, surely, she had tried to tell me something about this, even though the whole time we were there in Newtown together, she was talking about Sonya. Yes, even as we were sitting in that too-trendy café and then walking down Church Street towards where we used to live in Camperdown together – the three of us – and "happily", as she surprisingly said after everything she had been telling me about Sonya's view of things. And so, even as we were sitting side by side, on the lounges under those garishly upside-down, uddery cows in that Newtown café with our soft serve yoghurts and decaf cappuccinos, and then later while keeping to the narrow edge of Church Street as we walked along, beside the graveyard, hashing over our memories – that is, hashing only Sonya's view of our memories – on our way down to the park where we were going to sit and keep talking. In fact, it would have been *so* like the Eileen I have always known that even if she had been trying to tell me something important about herself, she had been working very hard instead to tell me about what was filling the mind of Sonya. The entire afternoon carrying on as if it were Sonya rather than her, Eileen, who was doing the talking. That all she was doing was laying herself down between us as if she, Eileen, were nothing more than an invisible figure – something like a "bridge" and "nothing more", as she even put it to me herself. In fact, I had told you in that Skype conversation, if you remember, that when Max had summoned me up to Katoomba by the state of his bewilderment and distress, I had told him that it was likely that Eileen was already, herself, "at a point of desperation", even though, as I also had to admit, I really couldn't account for why this thought had occurred to me then. Since the whole time I was with her in Newtown, it had been Sonya she had been talking about and so Sonya I had been thinking about – this channelling of Sonya, as I had called it for you – and for Max too – and so thinking about Eileen only insofar as she had been channelling Sonya and channelling me, as well, in the way I might have been as a person if I'd been so much nicer, and more careful and logical than I have ever been. It never having been possible to accept this version of me – this nicer version of me – without any protest on my behalf. This version that has always seemed to come along with the *other* version of me as well. As if there were two of me being addressed, or at least brought into being with her (Eileen): Sonya's version, and this other Eileen-ified version, of me. The last being completely false, the first unfortunately far too true, as I had only begun to suspect after I'd decided, once back in Sydney – in Chatswood – to ring for a skip. These various versions of me that you are always so keen to deflect as soon as I repeat them. It having been impossible to make you understand how I feel about these second-hand versions of me, since my confused feelings must be so hard for you to listen to, as well – impossible, too, since along with your justifications and dismissals of everything that you think has distressed me, you have your *own* version of how I am that takes no account whatsoever of how evasive I can also be. Yes, these many long years of abject evasions – my whole life, as it seems, intent on evading, and in fact succeeding in evading, what should probably be fundamental to my being as a daughter and a sister and a friend. Even as a human, as I once said to you that time we were in Suffolk, Teun, after we had sat staring out together at your car as it was being pelted by hail – "pelted onto an English crumpet", as you joked before you realised properly that I wasn't laughing with you but at your funny way of putting things. And so even though I have never managed to argue with what Eileen has always tended to say – or not so much say as imply, in every word that she uses when she's not forcefully putting forward, instead, what Sonya has got her to say – even though I have never been able to do this, I know I have definitely put my own, very pointed, but also entirely evasive, load across to her as well. The whole of it. Not taking issue with Eileen *per se* – I can never do that – but rather, always attempting to steer what I say in the direction that I want the whole conversation to go, and so in favour of some *other* version of my supposedly real intentions in something. Concocting this realness as I speak. This *other* layer of fiction. And hence the way that meeting up with Eileen in Newtown "so close to where the three of us had once lived together" had become *particularly weird* with her taking the part of Sonya, and me trying to get her to see things from my point of view, in relation to Son. Which of course she hadn't wanted to see – or at least, Sonya hadn't – the Sonya she was defending, as I had even gone so far as saying to Max by way of doing what I could to make up for what I'd said to him after seeing Lulu. *Particularly weird and strange.*

As I used the rest of the water in the bucket to slosh some grit off the porch, so that the channels branching from the corner to the steps thickened into ridges of wetted dust that I could pull with the end of a sort-of stick across to the furred-over saucers of geraniums by the treads – as I was doing all this, I kept going over in my mind how I had said to you, by way of asserting that I was fine and "even needed" up there in Katoomba, that Max was "out of his depth". That he was "flailing around with shock". And how I wished, too, as I also remembered thinking while I was still driving through the mist in the backstreets of Katoomba to get in some practice with the car – yes, even then, which is to say only early on in my journey "out west" towards Sonya – on this mission to find Sonya, and thus Eileen – how I wished that I was usually more *up front* with you about everything that happened to me. How, surely, for example, it should have been easy to say to you, then in Katoomba over Skype, that I had lost all interest, when I'd got the message from Max, in checking to see whether it was worth getting out dad's old car to drive it up there to see him. That, in fact, the thought of that car and my access to Eileen's place in the mountains was furthest from my mind. Because the moment that Max had contacted me, I started to panic. And yet I had wanted to help as well. In fact, I'd felt *obliged* to help, as I remembered trying, at least, to get you to understand over Skype when we were speaking in the café in Katoomba – remembering all this while I was driving Max's not quite so ancient but definitely more rusted and damp-smelling car back from the cliffs near Echo Point through a series of increasingly low-hanging hanks of mist – turning right into Lurline Street and then right again through the split-level road between Leura and Katoomba, which is to say moving in a highly circuitous way, since seemingly in the very *opposite* way, towards the ridge of Katoomba and, then, the highway. A circuitous way that was intended to give me a lot more practice on the gears and the clutch before heading out into *real traffic*, as I'd decided. Not at all trying to put the whole journey off, as it must have looked to anyone else – although it was also that. Helping rather than hindering me on my way to the ridge, where I would soon have to nudge this old bit of metal out onto the highway and then drive it directly west and then north in faster traffic. And so on my way to see Sonya, as I'd declared right at the beginning of the trip, to Max and his older two daughters who'd come down in their sleeping "dacks", as they called them, to see me off. And so, perhaps, yet another capitulation. Even then I was sure you would see it this way. And hence that statement I'd made to you earlier about my feelings – my wanting to-be-*generous* – my *friendly* feelings. That statement about my feelings that I'd readied, in defence, against my *refusal to take the car from the garage at dad's place*, as I had expected you to put it when I spoke to you over Skype towards the end of that first full day in Katoomba – that is, the day after I'd arrived there from Sydney. This pushing hard back, as if only to make up for what, to you, must have looked to be yet another extraordinarily stupid entanglement in Max and Eileen's and Sonya's lives – and one that I must surely have avoided, as I had then imagined you saying if we had been face to face and in the same small room (our London sitting room, say). And so driving Max's car that morning, through the moist and runnelled streets of Katoomba, the day *after* you had said to me so very clearly over Skype – after I started to tell you about "poor old Max and the girls", and how I'd had to get out to their place in Katoomba "as fast as I could". "No time to test dad's car". Remembering, as I drove about in the backstreets, how you'd said, then, that you had never expected me to drive dad's car *of course*. That a car of that age, and also that size, would have been difficult to manage. In fact, you would have advised against it except that you hadn't wanted to "kill off" what had seemed to be such an important thing for me – an important dream. Your not wanting to encourage me in the old car thing at all necessarily, but rather to advise against being dependent on others *yet again*. Your hope that I would at least *hire* a car if I wanted one – it being important to be independent, you'd said. Entirely independent. And really, that was all you had meant by saying what you'd said. Because the only reason you continued to worry about me in Australia was that at the slightest pull, at the very least cajoling, I shrivelled into a zombie-like pale and nerveless person – doing nothing but the will of others, as you have said on so many occasions, as if I were some frighteningly over-civil being. A terrifyingly abject thing – an automaton – and with no mind to call its own.

Because by now – yes, well after that conversation with you – that is, while I still was hunkered very tightly over the wheel of that car, and so early on in my journey out west – I could see that my response to Max about Lulu, and so about Eileen and Lulu, had been *definitely odd*. Thinking about it all over and over as I kept driving east towards Leura – which is to say apparently in the very wrong direction – before doing a slow, very dangerous three-point turn into a driveway on the long dipper street between Leura and Katoomba and then driving back up towards the centre of Katoomba again – past the ferns and the feathering rock-creeping leaves and tangles on either side of the street, where one side dropped away into a ditch of trees that was holding the mist up thick in their tips. I had said the *wrong thing* to Max, I know, I was thinking then in that car, and again – much later – in Chatswood, in Sydney. Almost saying it out loud as I decided to empty everything from the porch. To clear it out completely. The broken wicker chairs that were sending out spumes of sweetish mould, the dirt-filmed panes of glass that dad must have collected from somewhere. The newspapers (mostly local this time). All of the mail, trodden on which-a-ways. All of it down the stairs and onto the path and the lawn. The very wrong thing, I was muttering as I worked to keep on with what I was doing in clearing out the house like this. In fact, in the days after my conversation in the café with you, Teun, over Skype – that is, over the course of my journey out west – there and back – I became obsessed with how I had said the wrong thing to Max. Always the *wrong thing*. Always saying, precisely, the very thing that confirms, in its effects, what *you* have been worrying about in relation to all that I was likely to do or say over here. That would lay me open to being *taken over* – always being *taken over* – by other people's plans for me. And so all of this in my head as I drove, now, back in the right direction again – at last going west – driving up towards the roundabout that was at the top of the ridge at Katoomba. Shifting down the gears as I got closer and closer – soothed by the juddering, on-the-edge sound of the old crap gears that I was now definitely getting the hang of – only to come to a stop behind a van as a group of people – a large group of people – poured out from the top of the street towards the mouth of the station underpass. All of them young, in "trackies", as I used to call those outfits when I was still living here in Australia. Mullet-headed, metalled about the ears, lively and thick. One of them hopping forwards several paces on one crooked leg so that he could swivel back towards the others with his other leg held up high, his arms like the pinched-in talons of an insect. Like *this*, I thought I could hear him saying through the glass. And so thinking: even if I still went on to say to you or anyone else these twisted things – these very *wrong things* – this wasn't to say that I *didn't* have a backbone in me. Since Max hadn't exactly asked me *to do this*, Teun. *I'd* decided to do it. Really, it was only at that moment, as I waited for the kids to finish crossing the street so that I could keep on driving past the station in the centre of Katoomba, that I understood that what I'd done was to engage myself in a problem that was just as much mine as it was theirs. Because it had felt, for some reason, to be definitely mine as well. No matter that I couldn't admit it in so many words. And especially not to you over Skype (I'd realised), and let alone to Max or, really, anyone else. Yes, it had seemed at the time to be so much more genuine, or at least more *generous* – the way I'd hoped to be feeling – to say that once I'd seen Lulu I realised I needed to "focus" on the desperate plight of their family. That it was no longer just an issue of "poor anxious Max", as I'd been calling him the whole time for you when we'd been talking via our screens in the Katoomba café. Because I had come to realise that it had been odd – seriously odd – that when I had met up with Eileen in Newtown, instead of talking to her *properly* as I might have done – to this friend I hadn't seen for years – I had instead become obsessed with "my own bit of shit", as Son would have called it if it had been the other way around. My fury with Sonya's "supposed intervention", as I called it, after Nathaniel Lord's event at the Wharf. The way that Son had made sure that everyone on the night, indeed everyone over Facebook, would connect her disgusting intervention with me and my work. Her "pathetic intervention", as I probably called it too. That and the irritating way in which Eileen had taken Sonya's part in the whole of it – her willingness to pass on to me what she shouldn't have done if she'd wanted to hang on to herself as her own sort of person – a person who had her own sorts of thoughts, as she surely did. I should have said to you that I was annoyed, then, that with all this on my mind, I hadn't picked up on what must have been on Eileen's mind at the time. It being strange and worrying that I missed what instead should have been obvious and startlingly worrying – that is, whether my old friend Eileen had been about to split. About to freak. Was there a change in her tone as we talked? Any clue at all? Of course, you probably wouldn't have been, then, so very interested in this question of Eileen, Teun – not even of Lulu – I remembered thinking as the car moved forwards again at the crossing in Katoomba after the kids had passed. When I talked to you from that café in Katoomba over Skype before I left I might well have offered this problem of Eileen and Lulu, since it was still then so fresh. The whole problem of Eileen and the shock of her daughter's anorexia, and therefore what I had missed when I'd seen Eileen earlier that week. And so what, indeed, I should have noticed. What I might have said about it, too, if I had been a much better friend to Eileen than I usually was. But even if I had done this, I was realising, it was likely that you might have ignored it all the same – that you might still have gone back to the problem of the train and my "vulnerable position" in the mountains "with your lunatic friends". And so it might have been still necessary for me to say – the thought having occurred to me the moment I spoke it out loud in the car – this necessary defence – that I had actually enjoyed catching the train to the mountains this time. *The view is amazing from the moment you cross the river*, I could have said. From the river and the climb that follows – when you feel as if you've been lifted into some *other* place. The bit of Australia that I often think of with longing, I had thought but evidently not got round to saying to you. How it surprises me every time that I'm close to it. Even *this close*. On the other side of the glass. How all experiences like these are only ever reduced to such useless words as "amazing" and "longing". And so instead, I had told you how it had *felt right* to do what I was doing "up here". Because the fact was that it had indeed felt good – even right – to *be there* for Max and the kids. If only for Eileen's sake. Poor old Eileen, who now has a leg full of pins after running into the back of that truck down south – who won't be out of hospital and then "rehab", as they call it over here, for at least six months. All these years, Teun, I have been *slack*, as I so wish I had said to you in that café in my Oz sort of way. Never making an effort. Because, yes, I had been glad to see them again and glad, too, to be travelling towards them in Katoomba on the train rather than driving up the mountains in my father's, to be frank, *completely unroadworthy pile of seventies junk*, or indeed in any other car – in any other apparent sign of my independence, which can only ever be that: a sign only. Telling you, as I was remembering there in the car as I was nearing the last of the roundabouts before the entrance to the highway, how I had enjoyed the sudden surprise of the town itself. The mysterious way of it, where you step out from the ledge at the doors of the train onto the thinnest of platforms, on which everyone mills impossibly and then moves smoothly, practically slipping, down a long cold ramp under the rails – the small crowd of strangers that draws you up into the street there in Katoomba and then onto the peak of the slopes where, after one long and continuous fall, you will soon arrive at the cleft where Max and Eileen's house, pressing up on its precipitous southern border, looks out over the beginnings, as I've probably described it before, of what might have once been intended to be a street but is nothing but a dark and weedy section of part-cleared bush that I have always thought of as a local dump, at least since my first visit the year that mum died – it being "that kind of place", as I'd definitely said to you the last and so first time I had been to visit this "mountains retreat" of Eileen and Max's several years earlier but didn't want to repeat now that I had come up here after all, and *yet again*. And despite your warnings, Teun. Your well-meant warnings. And especially since it was clear that some-one had been repeatedly stuffing the putrefying contents of plastic bagged local newspapers and advertisements into the fence, where they gleamed in damp asphyxiation under the streetlights – repeatedly stuffing or rather, from another perspective, repeatedly ignoring that they were there. These rotting leavings of weeks if not months of neglected junk mail that were obviously just as impossible for Max and Eileen to remove and throw away as it had been the last time I was there. When the papers had seemed a lot greyer. So difficult, as it must have been for them, even when they'd arrived there newly keen – excited – to "deal with the shit" of the previous owners, as Max had called it. All of the crap that this owner had left in the garden, too, and which they'd had to push to the back of the garage as soon as they moved in. The shit in the house and the shit in the clearing of the bush beside it.

And yet there had been a change here all the same, I was thinking then as I drove from this last bit of village-scape – that is, driving along past the final roundabout in Katoomba, as Max had described it – driving for a bit alongside the railway line so I might evade the set of lights he thought might slow me down. So that I might, instead, slip out a lot more easily onto the highway. So that I might definitively start on this journey west to *sort it all out* with Eileen. Eileen and Sonya. Yes, a definite and positive change. Thinking about this, both in that car as I was driving along Bathurst Road beside the ditch of the railway line towards where I'd be able to slip onto the highway without having to stop anymore for a while, and yet again here in Chatswood even as I was beginning to realise that the series of loud, repeated beeps coming from a truck in front of the house meant that the bin was at last arriving. That it was at last being delivered through the gates out the front. Remembering how, this time at Eileen's place, I had noticed that, despite what I had seen with the local papers and letters still stuck in the fence, the section of land by the house was neater-looking – and had in fact been *substantially cleared*, as I tried to tell you that time in the café. Yes, I know I had made sure to tell you over Skype that there were no more piles of garbage bags now. No more toppled supermarket trolleys (I had said). No more softening chipboard bookcases or rusty wire or stiffened tyres filled to the tops of their rims with stagnant water – the bushy space alongside the house on the southern side having become quite a lot tidier now, wider even. Because a person or a machine had spread a thick layer of flesh-coloured bark chips over the weeds – perhaps Max or Eileen had done this. An immense effort to clean it up. This necessity to tell you something about all this. Anything, so long as it was positive then. This conjuring of the idea that it might have been Max or Eileen who had raked a truckload of tender bark chips over the rocks and the weeds and then rung up the council to remove the rubbish – even though, as I was talking to you then, over Skype in the Katoomba café, I also knew that it was *highly unlikely* that either Max or Eileen would have been up to doing such a thing, much as I would have loved them to be able to do so. Even just a little. The immense effort that it takes. An impossible effort, I was thinking again, as the truck kept beeping in the driveway at dad's place. And then the clanging of chains on metal. The long scrape of metal on concrete. And yet you would have guessed that it hadn't been Eileen or Max clearing the place at the side of their house anyway, no matter what I had tried to say to you then on their behalf. Still, the necessity to describe it – every one of the thoughts I have had about all of this. And only because there was nothing else, as I remember realising when I'd slipped out onto the highway and so towards Sonya – and Eileen too, as I still believed I was doing then (since this was well before I got the call from Max while I was sitting in the car by the giant funnels of Wallerawang, not sure what to do or even to think about after I'd taken in Sonya's rant from the phone call in Lithgow – when Max had rung me to head off my journey, to tell me the *unfortunate news* about the accident on the Princes Highway, which was much further south – as you need to realise – from where all of us were. This accident of Eileen's – a "prang", as Max had even called it at first). Only because there was nothing else I was going to be able to do then – then or now – other than to describe all this, one thing and then the other. And so the call from Max about the accident – this call that came in not even halfway along in my journey to Mudgee. This call that told me not too much about how Eileen was doing, since he didn't yet know a lot about what had happened to her leg. This call during which, at least, he told me that Eileen had been found and was mostly okay. But how it nevertheless brought the whole of it painfully close to me – it being far too difficult to believe that it wasn't, yet again, Leah being crushed under the metal of that car. Leah lying still, as I have always imagined it, but had never got to see for myself, obviously. Leah, this sister that had never made sense to me *as* a sister. This sister who had always kept away from me – from all of us – even when she lived here. When we were all in this house together. Judging every one of my draw-ings to be *fundamentally wanting*. Her criticisms, always, about everything that I did, which only made me work all the harder at my drawings to get her approval – perfecting my drawings. Everything for a smile of approval from her that, of course, never came. The way she would deliver her confus-ing barbs at the end of what might have been friendly chatter right up to that moment. Constantly the barbs. Picture it, Teun: a sister that, from the top of her crooked spine, turns a face towards you – a peculiarly impassive face – a face that is perhaps emotionless (as I'd always thought), but also perhaps one – as I can only begin to see now – only now begin to *take in* properly (and in the wake of everything that has happened over here) – a face that was probably always, and from the very beginning of my existence, pointed with hate or at least a poisonous envy that I was never able to see for what it was. Since why hadn't it been *my* spine in arthritic pain? as she might have wanted to ask me, but of course, never did. *My* compromised liver? *My* compromised spleen? Yes, I am describing all this for you in this document here, so you might have a chance to understand something of what is still so unclear to me, even now. And yet, how it might seem that I have lied to you about so many things over all these years. And that I keep on lying to you. Between the time that I leave this house, locked, dark and now chemical smelling, for the agents tomorrow – between now and my arrival back home in London – I am hoping you will at least have had time to start on this – so you might have begun to get even a small under-standing of why – as you have always put it – I have never been "rational" about my life over here. Why I seem to "persist" in ignoring all precautions, forgetting all precedents. "Continuing" to go against everything we "had discussed" after the last time I visited. That really, when it comes down to it, I have just done the *very* thing I told you in London I was *not* going to do on this trip to Australia to sort out dad's place. *Not* going to catch up with my art school friends. *Not* going to succumb *to the inevitable pressure.*

Acknowledgements

There are many, many people to whom I owe my warmest and most sincere thank yous for helping to shepherd this book out into the world, including Martin Shaw, Jim Gauer, Susan McCreery, Annee Lawrence, Bettina Kaiser, flowerville, Anna Gibbs, Magdalena Zolkos, Chris Peterson, Ed Wright, Shaun Prescott, Emily Hall, Mauro Javier Cárdenas, and of course my family – especially my very special and always encouraging partner in life Stephen Adams. I am also grateful to the Eleonor Dark Foundation for the opportunity of a week-long residency in the generative calm of Varuna early on in this novel's existence, almost before it had grown its own heart.

Extracts from this novel have appeared in the USA in *Denver Quarterly* and *Socrates on the Beach*, and for this I thank both Alicia Wright and Greg Gerke.

This novel was mostly written on Gadigal country, of the Eora nation, so I acknowledge the ongoing sovereignty of the traditional custodians of its lands and waters, and pay my respects to their elders past, present, and emerging.